HOPE IN THE MOONLIGHT

SHIFTERS OF MORWOOD: BOOK 2

CHARLENE PERRY

D1494488

HOPE

*S*ome days, I love my job.

He pushes cotton sweats down over lean thighs, and I struggle to keep my eyes safely fixed on the job at hand. His white briefs leave little to the imagination, and I can't help but note the sizeable bulge that's barely concealed.

"It's bigger than I expected... I mean... deep. Your wound's deep." Crap. Now I'm blushing.

"Yeah, it was my own fault."

Eddie hisses as I reapply pressure to his upper thigh. Some stitches and a shot of Medic, and he'll be well by morning.

"Do you want off wood chopping duty?"

"No." He clears his throat, perhaps a little self-conscious of my implication that he can't handle the job. "I'll be back to work first thing tomorrow. It was just a careless mistake. Won't happen again."

"Of course. You're all doing an amazing job." I give him an encouraging smile, and he seems to relax.

I press a damp cloth against his leg, carefully washing the area around the jagged wound. A shiver ghosts across my skin as I feel the moment he notices my touch in more than just a

I shake my head, reining in my wayward train of thought so I can get to work entering the details of his injury into his file.

With the day's tasks done, assuming no one else tries to chop their limbs off, I tug the tie out of my hair and run my fingers through the fine, pale length as it falls past my shoulders.

I love it here. I really do. The Meadow is small, but it's growing faster every year. As far as we know, it's the only place in the world where Shifter's live free of human control. Where we can be safe, raise families, and dream about a future when we won't have to live in hiding.

The Meadow is the heart of Morwood Forest, and the clinic is the heart of the Meadow. It's been my passion since I sutured my first laceration. Not simply for the medical aspect, though I enjoy that part. What I really love is the deeper connection this role gives me. The chance to mend a broken heart or ease a troubled mind. I know everyone who calls this place home, and they trust me with their most private concerns.

"Hope?"

Father's voice startles me out of my thoughts, and I jump up to look busy. I'm not sure why I bother. He never judges or pesters me. It's Mother who always seems to have one eye out for my lapses, and she rarely comes to the clinic thanks to her weak stomach for blood.

"I'm here."

"Oh, good. Good."

I meet him at the door, and he gives me one of his nervous smiles. He always seems a bit apologetic, but I suppose as a human mated to a Shifter, especially one as commanding as my mother, he's learned to tread carefully. I know he has a brave soul and a heart of gold under that quiet exterior.

If it weren't for my father, the Meadow probably wouldn't exist. Nearly thirty years ago, he worked at BioSol Labs. They tasked him with disposing of the so-called biological waste, which included the bodies of the female Shifters they euthanize after birth. He found my mother, a newborn wolf pup, still breathing amongst the pile. That heart of gold kicked in, and he snuck her home to nurse her back to health.

Naturally, she bonded with him. For a Shifter, that means she grew to match his biological age and maturity within six months. Then, in what I'm sure was a shocking moment for him, she took her human form.

That was when he discovered that Shifters aren't animals, despite what humans like to think. They made it their mission to save and awaken as many as possible, and with a small group in tow, they set out to live in safety off the grid.

Not long after that, I came along. The first natural-born Shifter.

For a long time, the Meadow was a mobile camp; always on the move and never too far from the cities for when we needed supplies. We found this spot about ten years ago, and it was too perfect to abandon.

"Your mother wants to see you."

I roll my eyes, and he responds with a stern glare that's almost comical on him. As much as my mother's a pain and a hard-ass, he loves her dearly and hates to see any sign that I'm disrespecting her.

"I'm not busy, Father. I'm coming." I glance behind me to make sure everything is tidy for tomorrow. Smoothing my hands over my shirt, I double check there's no trace of blood or other remnants of the day clinging to me.

I do respect Mother. She encouraged me to work at the clinic, even before I knew it was something I would enjoy. She's always coached me to wait for my true mate; for the one Shifter that's meant for me. She isn't the most affectionate mother, but she always has the best interests of the Meadow at heart.

I blink as I step out into the afternoon sun, the brisk breeze whipping my hair across my face. We walk the maze of packed dirt paths that snake between the tents, with Father glancing over his shoulder every few moments to assure himself I'm still following.

The sound of canvas flapping in the wind is a steady drone, and the cooks struggle to shelter their fires and keep up with the never-ending stream of demanding Shifter appetites.

Everyone here has a job and a purpose. Nobody's coerced or bribed. We all just do what we love and what we can for the Meadow.

There's a flash of emerald scales above, and I crane my neck to get a better view of Tarek as he flies in his dragon form. It's crazy to think a Shifter can learn to control such an incredibly powerful body. At least some of us can. Only the lab-grown variety.

As much as I try, it seems the natural-born Shifters are stuck with their inherited form. I can't even control my fur color, let alone my species. I never really cared before, but riding Damon's dragon makes me wish I could sprout my own wings. What a rush that would be!

"Hello, Mother." I greet her as I enter the spacious tent she shares with my father. I attempt to smooth my tangled hair after the windy walk, pulling it back into a high pony.

"Hello, daughter. It's so lovely to see you!" Her smile is wide, her teeth perfectly white against dark skin and thick, black hair. Her eyes dance with excitement.

Oh, crap. That's never the start of a conversation I'm going to enjoy.

GIDEON

"**C**an I help you with that?"

Just to prove I'm running on my last few brain cells, I slap my comm against the screen for the thousandth time. The same error message flashes yet again.

What the hell?

I tap it again, at a slightly different angle. As if that would fix the fact that those assholes pulled my credentials.

' Can't say I blame them. I've been showing all the signs of a man on the verge of a psychotic break.

I tap it again.

"Elite Gideon. May I help you?"

I look over at the pretty little blue-haired receptionist. Her signature smile, capable of lighting up a city, is replaced by a twisted mask of concern.

Fuck, I'm back to work for two minutes, and the rumors about my mental condition will be spreading. Not that they'll be false. How much can one person take before they break beyond repair? Not much more, I think.

"Yes, Dawn. Thank you."

When I use her name, that radiant smile returns. I realize

I'm smiling back. It's just impossible not to feel lighter around that girl.

"Where's Tarek today?"

She takes my comm and docks it with her tablet.

"He's been doing more wide patrols, with all the Horizon Zero business that went down. Just precautionary."

It's the standard line I give to anyone who notices his absence. Which is basically everyone I speak to, considering the massive green dragon was a landmark here on Solar One. It's better than telling them he broke his bond and ran off to join a covert Shifter colony.

"All good." She hands me back my comm. "Just a security update on our end. If it happens again, we can fix it up for you quick."

"You're an angel."

Her laugh is a mix of sweet and crazy. "Well, that might be a bit of a stretch. But you're welcome."

She gives me a wink before heading back to her desk. Always friendly, but never crossing into flirty. I wonder if it's just her work persona, or if she's like this all the time?

I shake my head. Time to stop stalling and face the music.

This is the first summons I've gotten from the Elders since everything went to shit with Camilla, so I'd better not fuck it up. That's assuming I even want to keep working as an Elite. Hell, I just don't know anymore.

If I can't protect the people I love most, how can I protect an entire city? But what good am I if I'm not a Protector? I don't exactly have a back-up plan if I fuck up this career.

I used to be filled with pride every time I walked through the doors of the Headquarters of the United Army of Terran Protectors. Lately, pride's the last thing I feel.

The elevator opens at the top floor of HQ, and I veer right instead of heading to the Atrium. There's nothing public about this meeting, not that they're holding much of anything publicly anymore. It doesn't convey much confidence to see four of the ten Elder seats empty, and people don't need a reminder of the corruption and lies that were so recently weeded out.

Elder Samuel sits behind his desk, in the center of a spacious office that looks more like a library than a workplace. His door's open, but I wait at the threshold for him to look up from his tablet.

"Elite Gideon, come in."

I step into the office, assuming an at-ease stance in front of his desk.

"My deepest condolences for the loss of your niece."

"Thank you, Elder."

"I trust you are well and able for duty?"

"Yes, Elder."

My reply is automatic. Serving the Elders is all I've ever done. All I've ever wanted to do.

As a boy, the Elites were my heroes. I knew them and their Shifters all by name. At seventeen, I applied to the Academy. A year too young, but by the time they discovered my age, I'd already obliterated the other applicant's scores. I graduated top of my class by a landslide. Skipped Enforcer and got an immediate posting as an Agent.

I was twenty-one when I requested promotion to Elite status. They laughed at someone my age for even thinking he had a chance. I was young and had more balls than brains, so I set my weapons to stun and walked through HQ. By the time I got to the Elder's inner offices, there was a trail of sleeping Protectors in my wake.

They could have had me executed for what I did, but I laid my weapons at their feet and gave them a well-rehearsed speech about how they needed me watching their backs. By some stroke of luck, the ridiculous fucking plan worked.

MATCH

"*I*t's lovely to see you as well, Mother." I breathe deep, coaxing my muscles to relax.

"How have things been at the clinic? The recent arrivals aren't taxing you too much, are they?"

"Fine. No, not at all." She waits, watching my face in that way she always does when my answer is too vague. "Most of them are healthy when they arrive. They just want to get settled in and look around. The wall construction is sending a little more work my way, but Brom's never far if I need a hand."

"Good. That's good."

She pauses, her eyes flicking to my father, who has settled down into his favorite chair to work on his latest carving. His hobby seems simple at first glance, but it's as important to the Meadow as any other task. An intricate bird is taking shape under his skilled knife, to be loved and enjoyed by the children for years to come. He started carving his toys when I was small, and I still remember the worlds and stories I created around them.

"Damon and his mate, they are happy to be reunited?"

"Yes. They are very much in love."

"That's wonderful. And you are content with his choice?"

"Of course. We're friends. I'm happy for them both."

"Excellent." She clasps her hands together in her lap. Her already perfect posture straightens even more as anticipation rolls off her in a thick wave. "Well, now that little diversion is behind us, it's time we got serious about your future."

My future?

"I'm perfectly content with my duties at the clinic..."

"Yes, yes. That's fine. Placing you with Brom was a wise decision. You've always been a natural." She picks at an invisible string on the hem of her white blouse, smoothing the front over her trim belly. "You'll be twenty-five soon, Hope. The Meadow is growing. It's time you took a mate worthy of you, to secure our position at the core of this community."

My eyes must widen to triple their normal size. My father coughs, keeping his gaze locked on his work. This is the first time I've heard anything like this from Mother. She's always coached me to wait for *the one*, always told me that when he arrives, I'll know.

Now it's time I *took* a mate? Sounds like we're about to plan an abduction.

A familiar tingle starts at the base of my spine as the Presence wakes. I take a slow, deep breath. There's no reason for me to be defensive. It's only a conversation.

"I haven't met him yet, Mother. I will-"

"Damon would have been an excellent match."

Heat rises in my cheeks. "Maybe, I mean, he's a good friend. But Whisper is his mate. He would never look for someone else. They're so in love. I truly understand now, why you always told me to wait. Love like that is worth waiting for."

She smiles, but it's a smile meant for a child.

"A Shifter that can control the form of a dragon would be a prize, indeed. Which is why Tarek will be an ideal choice."

"Tarek?" I choke on the word, but she's dead serious. The tingling rises a little higher along my spine. "I don't even know him. He comes with new Shifters, then leaves again. I've never met him in human form."

"It's no matter. He's here to stay for a while, to help with construction of the wall and new buildings. You'll get to meet him before the mating is made official."

The floor seems to tilt as my stomach takes a dive. I would think this was a joke, if Mother had a sense of humor. All those years of telling me to wait for the one, and what she meant was the one *she* chose?

Deep breaths. She's my mother, and my... leader. This is a conversation, not a life sentence.

"What if I don't like him? What if there's no spark?"

I look at my father again, but he's carving with intense concentration.

When the other teens were pairing off and exploring the concept of love, I waited. I didn't want to confuse lust with genuine love. When I became an adult, there were more options than just the natural children of the founding families. Lab-born Shifters who had been awakened, or rescued as young, were trickling in. I met a couple I liked enough to play around with, but I always kept it casual and brief, fearing that I would be distracted by the wrong playmate when my true mate came along.

"It's your duty to the Meadow. The other founding families produced offspring that can't hold a candle to your strength, intelligence or beauty. With a mate like Tarek at your side, they will never challenge our position as the head of our people." Her expression makes it clear the conversation is over, but my feet are frozen to the ground. She rolls her eyes, the way she's always done when my childish complaints bore her. "Tarek's already been informed. He's happy to do his duty to ensure the Meadow stays strong."

"Is it my duty to the Meadow, or my duty to you?"

The Presence flares to life, its energy surging along my spine to pool at the base of my skull. Ready. Waiting.

Mother's eyes burn into mine as she sucks in a breath. Her knuckles pale as she grips the arms of her wooden chair. I've never spoken to her that way; never challenged her wisdom or her devotion to our people. I swallow the guilt, allowing my selfish need for rebellion a moment to shine.

"I am the Meadow." She stands, walking toward me until her hands grip my shoulders. "And you are the Meadow. Your father started it all when he saved me."

"I know, Mother."

After my father realized the truth about Shifters, he told his friend, who was a Protector. Nathan woke his Shifter, Garret. Then Father woke Brom and saved three more females from the lab.

"Eight Alphas. Four founding families." Mother's hands still grip my shoulders as she looks at me like she's telling me something I haven't heard a million times before. "Love was never a requirement, though we have all been fortunate that love found us in its own time. Your father and I loved each other from the beginning, as did Nathan and Emily. Brom and Jasmine took a little longer to come together after their initial bond dissolved. Garret and Sadie despised each other once they were no longer bondmates, but they did their part to strengthen our community and love found them once they held their first young."

She looks almost caring as she stares into my eyes, compelling me to nod in agreement and push away my childish resistance. The Presence seems to calm, if only slightly.

"I know all this. You did what you set out to do. Now the Meadow is strong and growing faster each year. Everyone sees you as the head of the Alphas. I don't understand why my choice of mate will make any difference at all."

Mother's eyes leave mine for a moment as she looks to my father. She always looks to him like he might offer some wisdom, yet he remains content to follow her lead and offer nothing more than his presence as support.

"The four families produced thirteen young, including you and your brothers. Thirteen natural Shifters. The future of our species, independent of human intervention. Brom's daughters mated with two of Garret's sons, and they already have three grandchildren between them.

Leadership is strength. It's only natural that the strongest family will take the lead. You have a prominent role in the Meadow. You're strong, smart, and beautiful. If you're mated with someone like Tarek, no one will question our position."

I let out an unsteady breath, attempting to get my emotions under control. I need to be reasonable. Even if the thought of being unreasonable is beginning to feel pretty darn appealing.

"I don't think I can-"

"You're not a virgin, daughter."

I cringe as she says it like a medical fact. It's nothing we've ever talked about, but small community gossip and all that.

"No, of course not."

"Then you know there's nothing to fear. Besides..." She leans into my ear, her voice a whisper, "With a male like Tarek, it's not exactly a sacrifice, hmm?"

She's grinning when she pulls away, and I can't stop my expression from mirroring hers as I catch a spark of the excitement she feels at the thought.

It's all too ridiculous. This entire conversation. And yeah, playing around with Tarek would probably be a good time... but we're not talking about a casual fling. We're talking about mating and eventually producing young. We're talking about every hope and plan I've ever had about love.

Taking a mate.

Because it's best for the Meadow.

Reproduction. That's a whole other topic. Mother doesn't know about my defect. The Presence that lurks under my skin, invading the privacy of everyone around me when it pulls their emotions into my own. When it tingles up my spine and makes me think my body might not be only mine.

"I just need a little time to process-"

"We can't wait too long. I can't risk Garret making him a similar offer with one of his daughters. Particularly if she's more enthusiastic about the arrangement."

I close my eyes, but the Darkness waiting there seems far too animated to be benign. Instead, I look at Mother and offer a resigned smile that lets her know I'll be reasonable.

And I will be reasonable. I have to be, because this Presence inside me seems to like the alternative a little too much.

THIS IS ME

*O*h wow. That's a lot of male flesh.

The late afternoon is starting to cool, but Tarek's bare chest glistens as he hauls full logs beside a team of shirtless workers. He makes them look like children, with his immense shoulders and impossibly powerful arms. His face is rugged and handsome, his blond hair tied back. He looks like my father carved him out of wood, if my father were in the business of carving toys for adults.

He walks in the opposite direction, his body reshaping from one step to the next into his dragon. It's breathtaking to see such a powerful form wielded with such ease. He flies to the edge of the forest, gathers a mighty load of logs in his forearms, then returns to the construction and his human form.

The work will move a lot faster with him on duty.

I steel my confidence, walking closer, and it's only a moment before he notices me. His smile is genuine and even, his teeth white and straight. When he leaves his work to join me, a shiver of anticipation ripples over my skin. I might not like that this decision is being taken from me, but the thought of having this particular male's attention isn't so unappealing.

"Hope." His voice is deep, almost gravelly, and the sound of my name on his tongue is hardly unpleasant.

"Tarek. I wanted to introduce myself."

He nods, his emerald eyes traveling over me in a blatant inspection. Heat rises in my cheeks as I wonder what Mother would have told him about me.

"So, ah, my Mother thinks we'd make a good couple." That might be the strangest sentence I've ever heard myself say.

"I'm grateful for the life I've been given, and I'm in debt to the Meadow. I'll gladly serve in whatever way is most helpful."

A hint of color touches his cheeks, and I can't deny I'm attracted to him. I'm also pissed off.

I'll gladly serve. Isn't that the story of my life? I love my work at the clinic, but I'm there because Mother decided it was how I could best serve the Meadow. Probably because the position comes with a status that makes her look good.

I bought her love story, too. The one where my true mate shows himself at the right moment, when all she intended was for me to wait until she found someone she approved of.

Isn't the point of the Meadow that Shifters can live their lives, free of human control? I might not be bonded with a human, but I've been living as her willing puppet for my entire life. Have I ever had an original thought that wasn't first planted there by her?

Maybe I should tell her the truth; that her precious, natural, pure Shifter progeny is defective. That it's all a lie. That every good thing I do is my way of fighting off the Presence crawling under my skin.

I take a breath and unclench my fists. I thought I left all this frustration back in Mother's tent, but I guess my temper isn't done resisting just yet.

"It was good to meet you, Tarek."

I give him a stiff smile, and he widens his.

There's no point in bothering him with my inner turmoil. With a nod, he returns to his work. I look around me, at the construction of new, permanent homes. At the wood being cleared to expand the Meadow, and the evidence of the wall's construction beyond the tree-line.

This isn't the time to be having a childish rebellion. Whether I like it or not, the Meadow must come first. My duty to the Meadow must come before my own silly fantasies.

"Hey! Hope!"

River's voice instantly lightens my mood. I turn away from the view of Tarek and embrace my friend.

"Hey, Riv. I thought you were on patrol today?"

"Nah, yesterday. I'll be glad when the wall's done, so we can stop running around like animals in the forest." She shudders, and I roll my eyes. She knows I love my wolf, but River would be content never taking her lioness form. "So, Damon and Whisper had quite the reunion. I was still rooting for the two of you to hook up."

"River!"

"I know, I know. We're all happy for them. But still, you two were totally adorable together."

"It was never a thing."

"I know. Relax. And check out this view..."

I follow her gaze, already guessing whose shirtless form it's locked on. I wonder if there really is a chance that Garret will try to convince Tarek to take one of his daughters instead. River is quite a catch, and her older sister, Daisy, is ready and eager to settle down.

"He's something, all right."

River doesn't miss my awkward reply. When I look back at her, she narrows her eyes and waits. She knows the silence will get me talking faster than pointed questioning.

"It's nothing. I'm fine."

Hell, a few years back I would have had a woman like that on her back in a heartbeat. But that was before Lily.

Whisper was the closest I've come to that mistake in a long time. Fuck, but that woman can break a man with one look. It was an act of sheer willpower to keep my hands off her. That would have been all kinds of bad news, particularly once Damon decided to upgrade from her partner to her lover. Not a man I would want to be in competition with.

"You okay, hon?"

"Yeah."

I hold my empty glass out, not surprised that Kelsey already has the bottle open. The back room is empty tonight, the tv tuned to local news and coverage of the election.

Tanikka Durant's face is front and center, as she gets encouragingly close to the finals. She stands out like a beacon of potential among the typical lineup of aging, morals-for-hire men. She's the change we need.

With her as an Elder, women might have an easier time climbing the ladders in work and government. Maybe Shifters will have a shot at being recognized as more than just property.

Kelsey finishes pouring my drink, then sets the bottle on the edge of the old pool table. She runs her fingers over its worn green surface as she stares toward the tv.

I want to tell her that Whisper is alive and well. She's taking a risk by welcoming Shifters here and keeping their secret. She would keep Whisp's, too, but it's not my place.

"It might do you good to say yes once in a while," she says. "You deserve a little fun, and Madison's definitely fun."

"I'm saving myself for you, Kelsey, you know that."

"Honey, if you keep this up, I might just take you up on that out of sheer pity."

"I don't see you taking any women home, either. Fuck knows you get more offers than anyone."

"I don't mix business and pleasure, but don't you worry about me. My bed's always warm."

"I guess I'll just keep waiting for you, then."

She pats me on the arm. My comm vibrates in my back pocket, and I pull up the message on my neural interface through my Comm implant.

"Cabs here. Gotta run."

"Okay. Be safe."

"I'm taking a bit of a vacation. Heading into Morwood for a hike."

"Oh! How classically masculine of you."

"Yeah, well, I'm a classically masculine kind of guy. Take care of Tarek if he stops by while I'm gone. Keep his tab open, but make sure he doesn't do anything stupid."

"As always."

"And be careful. What you're doing here is important, but if you get caught-"

"We're not married yet, Gideon. Stop nagging me."

In the blink of an eye, I've got her pinned against me. My free hand covers her mouth. She struggles, but it's entirely futile. With her back against me and my arm securing hers against her sides, she's helpless to gain any leverage.

I don't tap into my Stim implant often. Fuck, it's a heavy rush.

"That's how fast shit will get out of your control if they find out about this place and send someone like me." I remove my hand from her mouth, but I want to make sure she's not in attack mode before I release the rest of her. "I'll be out of contact while I'm gone, so I won't be able to help if anything happens."

She doesn't respond, so I release her and step back a few paces. She adjusts her clothes as she turns to face me again, her eyes focusing anywhere but on me.

"You're important, Kelsey. To me and to Whisper."

"Thank you, Gideon." She looks up at me, and I see a rare vulnerability in her eyes. "I don't know why you care so much, but I appreciate it. Thank you. I'll be careful."

I nod, giving her a friendly punch in the shoulder as I head out to catch my cab.

Fuck, I'm getting attached to that woman. She's impossible not to like, and she's risking everything to help Shifters. Thank fuck she's not into men. Just a simple friendship without any complications.

I need a good, long break from complications.

PATROL

*W*hen I roll off my cot at daybreak, I'm bleary from a restless night. I can't stop thinking about the conversation with Mother, and about Tarek.

The last few days have been ordinary in every way. A few minor injuries to tend, a new baby born, some routine follow-ups. A lot of cataloging and organizing. All the day-to-day stuff that fills my time and defines my role in the Meadow.

I don't let my personal issues affect my duties, but when the days are done and I'm alone in my tent, the uncertainties and fears consume me.

I shake out my fur and shift to my human form. My worn jeans and lavender sleeveless are crisp and clean; a handy side effect of shifting. I pull off the shirt, replacing it with a pastel yellow version.

Out on the path, I move at a brisk pace. The sun's only just beginning to light the still morning, but already the scent of cook-fires and the sounds of construction greet me with the promise of progress and a full belly.

The wall is sprouting up around our perimeter, growing out of the forest more and more with each passing day. It's an impressive undertaking, but it reminds me just how vulnerable we've been without it.

We've kept to ourselves in the past. Other than a few brave Shifters living as humans in the city, and our necessary trips to collect supplies, we've been isolated here together. Now, with the increase in Shifters being awakened to leave their Protectors and join us, it's only a matter of time before the humans catch on.

It's definitely no time to be thinking about something as selfish as love.

Once I check in to make sure I'm not needed at the clinic, I'll be off for the day to take my turn on patrol. As much as I love my work, I might enjoy my patrols even more. On four legs, with my wolf's speed and heightened senses, I'm connected to the earth and to a part of my soul I can't quite define. If it weren't for the clinic, I'd probably spend most of my time in my wolf's body.

I push through the heavy canvass and say a quick *good morning* to Brom.

"You just can't take a day off, can you?"

"Of course I can, I-"

"When's the last time you went one full day without sticking your nose through that door?"

I cross my arms and attempt to look irritated, but the old cougar Shifter just laughs. It's pointless to argue when he's in the mood to tease.

"You know, I was running this clinic just fine long before you came along. I think I can manage a day or two on my own now and then."

Brom started this clinic when the Meadow was brand new. He taught me everything I know, and eventually stepped back to let me take the lead, though he's never far when I need a hand.

"The Meadow was a lot smaller back then, and it took me eons to get this place organized. Who knows what mess I'd come back to if I left you alone?"

Brom laughs again, his weathered face crinkling as he waves me off.

The issues we deal with here are few and simple enough, and I certainly don't question his medical skills. He just doesn't have the same connection with our people that I do. It's not him they turn to with wounds that are more than just physical. Besides, maintaining the equipment and cataloging fresh supplies as they're smuggled in from BioSol or Moridian is almost as much fun as tending the patients.

I don't take a day off, because I don't want a day off.

My next stop is Sadie's cookfire, and I'm ecstatic to find Damon and Whisper are already there, huddled on a log bench and eating the eggs and deer steak being offered up by River's mother.

"Look who decided to join the world," I say after I grab a plate of steaming food. They both look up, matching grins on their happy faces. It's infectious, and I can't help but grin back.

"Morning, Hope," Whisper says as I settle onto the ground in front of them.

Damon cups his hand around my head and plants a warm kiss on my forehead. I peek at Whisper, but she's still all smiles.

I don't know her at all, but Damon's devotion and his obvious joy at having her back makes me feel like we're already friends. She scoots over, making space for me between them on the log. Tears sting the back of my eyes at the kind gesture.

I think the friendship that grew between Damon and I in her absence would threaten most females. They wouldn't want me anywhere near their mate. Not Whisper. If she has any reservations, she trusts Damon's heart enough to ignore them. I haven't lost a friend, I've gained another.

"Thank you."

Whisper nods, her eyes telling me she understands I'm thanking her for more than just a seat.

The three of us eat in silence for a while, but when their plates are clean, I set mine on my lap and take a deep breath.

"Whisper, how did you know Damon was the one?"

Damon chokes on a laugh. "She didn't. It took a hell of a lot of convincing. Fuck, I had to die for her to finally get it."

I look back at Whisper, and although she's smiling, it doesn't reach her eyes. She looks almost sad.

"But you two are obviously meant for each other."

Whisper's face is serious as she holds my stare. Then she looks past me, at Damon, and I get the feeling her words are meant more for him.

"He was my partner. My best friend. When he took human form, I was convinced it was unnatural. Even when he showed me how right it was, I was still in denial. I couldn't fight the chemistry, and I felt the love, but I was so convinced it was wrong that I ignored it. I thought it wasn't real."

"I've always loved her, but it changed when I took human form. Once I knew our bond was broken, I knew my emotions were my own."

That's not the least bit encouraging. These two are perfect for each other, and they didn't even know it for, well, years. I finish my steak, then stand and brush off the seat of my pants.

"Is everything okay?" Whisper stands with me, her hand touching my arm for a moment before pulling away.

"Yeah, for sure. I'm just..." I stop myself. There's no need to trouble them with my little issues. "... I'm good."

"Done with your dishes, loves?" Sadie's cheery voice is a

welcome distraction, and we hand over our plates with sincere thanks for the meal.

"Sadie, have you met Damon's mate, Whisper?"

The matronly lioness Shifter balances the plates in one hand so she can offer the other in greeting.

"It's good to meet you, love. And wonderful to see your brooding panther with a permanent smile on his face." Sadie winks as Whisper beams.

"Thank you. It's great to meet you, too."

"Sadie and her mate, Garret, are two of the original founders of the Meadow."

"It's true. Hope's father got me out when I was just a cub, about a year after he saved Molly. He gave me to that handsome leopard over there." She tips her head toward Garret in his usual position, mending a torn canvas from someone's tent. "They didn't know for sure if the bond would work between two Shifters, but it turned out just fine.

Anyway, loves, cooking is my true passion these days. So anytime you're hungry, you can find me here or in the gardens. I'm too old for hunting for much more than herbs."

She laughs, giving my arm a squeeze before returning to her chores.

"Everyone's story is so unique, their lives so..." Whisper's voice trails off, but I understand her meaning.

"It's a different way of looking at a life," I say. "Sadie isn't much older than I am, if you count her years. She's lab-born, so by the time she was six months old she had aged to match Garret's forty years. So, she's about sixty-five now, even though she was born twenty-five years ago. Garret had only been alive for fifteen years, but his Agent was twenty-five when they were matched."

Whisper's quiet, but her hand reaches out to grasp Damon's. It must be quite a change for her, coming from the life she lived as an Agent. It's time to head out for my patrol, but I don't want to leave yet, in case she has more questions.

I find it all so fascinating; the differences and similarities between Shifters and humans. I've even been doing a bit of experimenting with blood samples, learning some interesting things and discovering I might have a little scientist in me.

Damon growls, a territorial tone that tells me a certain golden wolf is approaching.

"It's fine. We're on patrol today."

"Why does your mother..." He stops the sentence before he finishes his thought. Like the true Meadow resident he's become, even if he doesn't agree with her he has too much respect to voice it.

I hear a low growl behind me, and I turn as Luke takes his human form. He's attractive, with his yellow-green eyes and thick, blond hair. His body is fit and always on display with those thin, drawstring pants he wears. He'd be content running around naked, I'm sure.

Damon steps up, the two males going toe-to-toe. Their disdain for each other is palpable, and completely my fault. Well, Luke's fault too, for being a general ass.

"Guys, stop. Damon, it's fine. Really."

I glance at Whisper, who's eyebrows are raised in curiosity, a slight smirk on her face.

"Let's go, Luke. We're already late relieving the others."

I don't bother waiting for a response as I shift to my white wolf and lope toward the forest.

WHISPER

I put my hand on Damon's shoulder, feeling the tension in his body. He's itching to put Luke in his place, but he's too level-headed to start a fight.

"Hey, Luke," I say, my tone a lot friendlier than the situation calls for.

It gets his attention, and he looks away from the silent pissing-contest they're having to meet my eyes. He gives me a once-over, clearly finding me to be no threat.

"Whisper," he nods, almost friendly if it weren't for the set of his jaw and the fire in his eyes. "Keeping your pet in check, are you?"

I laugh, squeezing Damon's arm so he doesn't do something stupid. I push between them, getting nice and close so only Luke can hear me. "Oh honey, he's no pet. And I'd love to see him put you on your ass. Again."

Luke growls, not sounding so tough with me standing chest-to-chest. I grab the knotted string that's barely holding his pants up, giving it a little tug. "How about this? You want to fight, just say the word and the two of you can take it outside the village. I have no doubt Damon could put you down within two minutes. But if you insult Hope, if you so much as look at her without her permission, I'll come find you when it's nice and quiet. I've got a few creative ways to make sure you never think about forcing yourself on a woman ever again."

That makes his breath stutter, as the last of his cocky expression disappears.

Damon grips my arms, pulling me back. I keep eye contact with Luke, licking my lips. He shifts into a golden wolf and flashes his teeth before loping after Hope.

"What did you say to him?"

"Just enough to get his imagination working."

Damon knows me well enough not to ask for details he doesn't really want to have.

"How about we go back to the tent?"

I laugh. "I've hardly seen more than the inside of that tent since I got here."

He growls, pulling me tight against him. A flush of uncertainty washes over me at the thought of how many people are around us. A few curious eyes stare, though most are going about their business without concern for us.

We've had to keep our relationship secret since it began, the consequences of being discovered too severe to risk. The knowledge that we're safe here, free to be ourselves and be together, will take some getting used to.

"I can show you the hot springs." His breath is hot against my ear as his arousal hardens against my belly. "Or the clearing at the top of the north mountain..."

"Fuck off, Damon. My vagina needs a break."

He growls, nipping a path from my ear down my neck. Shivers ripple across my skin, and I'm not so sure I need a break after all. Fuck, we've had sex more times over the last few days then I can count. More than I've had in my entire life.

"Okay. I'll show you around." He pulls me in for a quick

kiss. "But first, I've got to make an appearance at the wall. I'm not going to be a very useful member of this community if I don't start making use of myself again."

He grabs my hand, pulling me with him as he walks.

I'm such a hypocrite. I should appreciate that he's respecting my need for a break, but instead I'm disappointed he didn't opt for throwing me over his shoulder and taking me away. Shaking my head, I attempt to get my brain back online.

A useful member of this community. Since I arrived a few days ago, I've been attached to Damon. Literally, for the most part. But I'm not cut out to just be someone's *mate*. It might be a fun role for now, with nothing to worry about other than the way we make each other feel, but it's not who I am.

We pass another cook fire, this one tended by an older man. Everything here has a use, and every person has a job. I love to cook, but I'm more of a gourmet oven chef than the open-fire variety. Besides, it doesn't really sound appealing to spend my days cooking and serving. I hate sewing. I can haul wood and build, but that seems to be more the territory of the males, and the thought of spending my days beside a crew of sweaty, shirt-less... okay that one sounds kind of appealing.

A pained yelp pulls my attention to an open patch of grass at the edge of the tents, where two young men are sparring. It's clearly a friendly fight, but they seem to be getting increasingly heated as punches and kicks slip by poorly planned blocks.

"Give me a minute, Damon."

He drops my hand, and I skip off the path to approach the fighters.

"Hey, boys."

That grabs their attention fast, since they're both old enough not to be called boys, but young enough to get offended when someone does. They look at me, then at each other. Damon must follow me, because one of them nods over my shoulder.

"Whisper." The biggest says my name in greeting, even though he's never laid eyes on me before now. Small town gossip.

"Are you practicing?"

He puffs out his chest. "Yeah. It's good to keep in shape, in case we need to defend the Meadow from humans."

"I'm a human."

His face turns red. "I didn't mean-"

"Hit me."

He steps back, his eyes snapping over my shoulder to the likely smiling Damon. "I didn't mean it like that. You're not-"

"It's okay. I have a little hand-to-hand experience, and I wouldn't mind the practice. If you don't want to hit me, just knock me off my feet. See if I can dodge you."

"I wouldn't want to hurt you."

"I'm half your size. There's no need to be scared."

His eyes darken, as his buddy covers a grin.

"If we're attacked by humans, and you can't even take out a little female..."

He growls, and I know I've hooked him. Still, he looks past me at Damon.

"Go for it," Damon says, and I can hear the laugh beneath his words. "Show her she's not as tough as she thinks she is."

That's all the encouragement needed, and he digs in for a solid charge. Half a second later, he's on his back, his own momentum doing all the hard work. Basic shit.

I stand over him, ignoring the hysterical laughter of his friend. He's red-faced and breathing heavy, trying to process what just happened. I hold out my hand to offer assistance, but he growls and rolls to his feet. I turn my attention to his laughing friend.

"Think you can do better, big guy?"

He doesn't hesitate, just comes at me swinging. A last-minute dodge-and-spin, and I've got his legs out from under him. He lands on his face in nearly the same spot his friend did. I poke at his ribs with my foot, and he scrambles to his feet.

I raise my hands in surrender.

"Do you have implants?" The first guy tilts his head as he looks at my bare neck.

I rub the place where my tats used to be. "No. I have experience, and proper training. When you can't rely on brute strength, you have to be smarter and more coordinated. What's your names?"

"Haden."

"Theo."

They both look a bit smaller than when I first approached, their confidence taken down a few pegs. If this is what the Meadow has to offer for fighters...

I look back at Damon, and I'm sure he knows what I'm thinking. I can use my combat skills to contribute something important to the Meadow.

He steps closer to me, cupping my cheek and giving me a quick kiss. His hand slides down to rest on my belly.

"Do you think you should-"

"Don't go there."

I know what he's thinking, too, and I don't want to hear it. My Medic was my birth control, and it's been gone since before our night in the birch trees at Tobias' estate. I hadn't given it any consideration at the time, not expecting to live much longer, anyway.

I'm confident that I didn't get knocked up back then, but after the last few days... I should have been smarter. I need to talk to Hope and see what they have here for options.

Not that having a family with Damon doesn't sound like a dream, just not yet.

"Don't hurt them, ok?"

He's letting the issue rest for now, but I know it's far from out of his mind.

"I'll try not to."

MOONLIGHT

*M*y legs are burning and my stomach is rumbling by the time the sun begins to set. I spent the morning with Luke, weaving through trees in an expanding loop around the Meadow. He was oddly quiet, and never once shifted to human form. By midday, our loops were far enough from the Meadow that we split up to cover more ground.

The darkening sky says it's time to head back, but I'm not quite ready yet. I like it out here, alone in my wolf's body. And I'm so close to my favorite place in the world.

I head farther from the Meadow, following the sun's retreat, until the forest stops at the edge of Moonlight Lake. I only come here at night, when everyone else is huddled around cook-fires or relaxing after a long day. Every time I step onto the rocky ledges above the still water, I'm taken aback by the incomparable natural beauty of this place. It takes my breath away.

The dense forest behind me ends at the edge of a cliff, a twenty-foot drop to the rocky shore below. To my left and on the opposite side of the lake are snow-peaked mountains and more rocky cliffs. To my right, the approach is a little gentler, with thick trees and heavy brush tapering into soft, mossy earth and a little sandy swatch of beach.

The sun sinks low over the mountains, casting the lake in brilliant pink and purple hues. The best part comes when the last of the sun's light is gone, leaving only the moon to reflect its eerie silver light. Tonight, it's full in a clear, starry sky.

I settle down onto my belly. I'll stay here tonight. No one ever notices I'm gone, as long as I return before morning.

I attempt to clear my mind and simply be at peace with the landscape, but my churning thoughts are relentless even here.

The Meadow needs me. My people need me. I don't fully understand Mother's methods or reasoning, but that doesn't mean I know better. If being Tarek's mate is the best thing for our future, then I should be happy to have him.

But what about Tarek's opinion? He's new and eager to do his part for the Meadow, but can I let him agree without telling him the full truth? How would I even start?

Oh, by the way, I might be a natural Shifter, but I've got something very unnatural gaining strength inside me. I actually might be evil. I'm sure it won't be a problem.

Oh, blazes. I can't tell him. I can't tell anyone.

If my choices are so important to Mother's position among the Alphas, what would it do to her if anyone found out how defective I am? But it's not like I haven't been able to hide it so far. It might be getting stronger, but I can still keep it under control.

No one has to know, ever.

The full moon rises higher over the mountains and bathes my world in silver. A nervous deer and her wobbly fawn emerge from the trees, testing the air as they approach the water. She catches my scent, and they bolt back to the safety of the forest.

An urge strikes me, one I often feel under the moon but

rarely indulge. I push up to my haunches, tip my head back, and howl. Long and melodic, it isn't long before my tune is picked up by the wild wolves that inhabit the forest. I never see them. They know I'm not one of them even when I'm in this form. But as our voices mingle, a distant kinship tugs at my soul.

When the primal call wanes, and the replies fade into the night, I open my eyes. Movement catches my attention. I snap my head to the beach below and see a man carrying a heavy backpack that he heaves onto the ground just at the edge of the sandy beach. He's wearing a light jacket, grey shirt, cargo pants in a camouflaged pattern, and boots that appear too heavy to be comfortable.

He's looking right at me.

That silly howl announced my presence well before I noticed he was here. What's a human doing this far into Morwood? I'm certain he's human, because no Shifter would weigh himself down with such clothes and gear.

I turn to face him, keeping my head and ears up so he can see I'm only curious. His pale eyes shine in the moonlight. His short hair is messy, his shoulders wide, and his chest thick. He's obviously fit, with a face attractive enough to hold any female's attention.

Keeping his eyes on me, he turns his head and tips his neck just enough that I can see dark markings against his skin. I can't make out the details from here, but a trail of tattoos runs from behind his ear, down to his collarbone.

He's an Agent. No, with that many tattoos, he's an Elite.

I feel my lips peel back from long fangs, as my ears flatten and my head and tail lower. My wolf instincts are reacting to the threat even before I've fully processed it. An Elite this close to the Meadow... a few hours run for me, a day's walk for him.

I can't let him get any closer.

~

THIS IS a sight I won't soon forget.

The wolf's howl was too close not to investigate, and the scene before me now is breathtaking. A still lake in the middle of the dense forest, guarded by ragged cliffs and snow-peaked mountains. On a ledge overhanging a small, sandy beach, a white wolf sits with its head thrown back, howling into the night.

The full moon frames it in silver light, casting its face in shadow. When it stops the eerie song, it turns toward me and I'm certain it's no ordinary wolf. It's a Shifter.

I keep my eyes on it as I tip my head, showing my tats. Its curious demeanor melts into a defensive display, as a throaty growl fills the silence.

I sit on my backpack, hoping to appear as less of a threat. I shrug off my jacket, rolling my sleeves up to my elbows. He's a big one, but I'm no lightweight.

"I take it I'm close to the Meadow?"

The growling stops.

"I'm here to talk to a friend. I have a message. A warning. I know I'm going in the right direction, but I don't know how far away I am."

My link with Tarek still works, but so far he hasn't answered. I don't want to give the wolf more information, but as the minutes pass by in silence, I'm fairly certain he doesn't plan to point me to the Meadow.

"Okay, fair enough." Standing up, I move with deliberate slowness to avoid spooking him. "I was planning to make camp here anyway, so you can keep me company if you like."

I unpack my bedroll and a few basic odds and ends. Not too much that I can't grab it all and make a quick exit if needed. I gather dry wood and brush to set up a proper campfire, then unroll my bed onto the mossy ground cover at the edge of the sand.

The wolf just watches.

As eager as I was to get some time away from people, two weeks in the bush has reminded me that being alone with my thoughts isn't always preferable. The company of a Shifter is something I've missed since Tarek woke.

"Mind if I light it?" I look up at him, but the moonlight still leaves his features in shadow. "It's cold for a human, but if you think it wouldn't be wise-"

With effortless leaps, he's off the ledge and loping toward me. I brace myself, resisting the urge to reach for the knife strapped to my thigh. He stops a few meters away, and when he looks up at me, it's with the strangest eyes I've ever seen. They're almost purple against his white coat.

It's still strange to think about Shifters taking human form. I'm looking at him, appreciating the strength and beauty of the wolf in front of me in a way that I would never consider if he were in his human form. I look away and clear my throat.

"So, is that a yes to the fire?"

He makes a noise like a sharp growl, then moves to settle down on his belly at the opposite side of the pile.

"Okay then."

A few moments later, there's a small blaze going. Just enough for a little warmth.

"I've been hiking through Morwood for a couple weeks now. It's nice to have some company."

Those violet eyes watch me through the firelight, obvious intelligence despite the animal body. Watching him as he watches me, I can't help but wonder about his story. Was he a Protector? I don't think I've ever seen a wolf like him around. Those eyes alone would have made a lasting impression. Was he born out here? Tarek talked about natural Shifters, born in the Meadow instead of the lab.

"Were you a Protector?"

The wolf moves his head from side to side in an obvious 'no'. I'm not sure why, but the next question makes my heart beat a little faster.

"Were you born out here? Are you a natural Shifter?"

He nods, never taking his eyes off mine.

"That's... awesome."

I don't know why I feel so affected by the idea; by the fact that his kind can exist on their own. Maybe because I spent so many years viewing them as human property.

I look away, out at the moonlit lake instead of into those intelligent eyes. After a moment, I settle onto my back, folding my arms behind my head.

I can still sense him watching me.

"It's all kinds of fucked up, isn't it?"

He growls.

"For what it's worth, I'm sorry for what we've done to your kind."

I think he stops breathing for a minute, but then he heaves a heavy sigh. I get the impression that even if he's been out here his whole life, he hasn't been immune to the consequences of the Shifter program.

I'll just have to hope he decides to trust me regardless of his opinions of my species. Getting closer to the Meadow without his permission is unlikely, and the thought of forcing my way past him sits in my gut like poison.

COMPANIONS

I can't stop watching him. I know it's wrong, but I've never seen a man, let alone a *human* man, so unguarded. It's like the moment when I first walk into a room, before they realize a female is present. They behave differently in small ways.

And he honestly has no idea I'm female.

When he woke up with the sun, he stretched, scratched his man-bits, and promptly announced he needed to take a piss. Then he did. On the nearest tree. Not that I could see anything, but I could hear it. He washed his hands at the water's edge, opened up more of his supplies, and made a breakfast of canned soup.

He offered to share, but I refused. I'm hungry, but I've never cared much for eating in this form.

"The water's warmer than I expected for this time of year."

I find it interesting that he talks to me like that. Small talk. Little comments about random things, even though he's aware I can't respond in this form.

I start to sit up before catching myself. I don't want him to see that I'm not a male. It's dishonest, but I'm not ready to break this spell just yet. Or to lose the ability to watch his every movement without seeming rude or creepy.

He goes about his business without suspecting how much I'm enjoying the way his muscular body moves beneath his clothing. The way his forearms flex with taut muscle, or the way his thighs stretch the limits of his pants when he crouches... this man is all sorts of daydream fuel.

I should have returned home before dawn. My absence at the clinic is bound to be noticed soon, but I can't leave yet. And not only because I'm enjoying his company and the chance to observe him so openly. I'm also well aware that he can't be allowed to discover the Meadow's location. I'm hoping he'll tell me the message he needs to deliver and then turn back the way he came.

He stands up from his spot by the campfire, and I'm shameless as I watch him stretch, the sound of a joint popping followed by a satisfied grunt. He reaches over his head, grasps his shirt between his shoulder blades, and he pulls it up.

Oh... crap.

Time slows to a crawl as the hem of his shirt slides up, revealing inch by inch of smooth, male flesh. The v-cut of his hips, his navel, deeply defined abs, a broad, wickedly contoured chest... When the fabric is fully peeled off, his bare torso is framed by wide shoulders and thick, strong arms.

I can't tear my eyes off him. I don't think my mouth is capable of closing. I've seen plenty of shirtless males, but this human... every line and every muscle was sculpted by sheer physical effort. He didn't just shift into this body, he worked for every curve.

I need to shift. Or I need to go. I can't...

His hand is on his belt. He flips the clasp with ease, pops the button on his pants, and lowers the zipper.

It's so wrong that I'm still watching.

He pushes his pants down over his hips. Over his thick thighs. He's wearing tight boxers that cling to his flesh like a second skin. The bulge in the front of them is huge... I've never...

I close my eyes and turn my head. This is wrong. I can't take advantage of this, or of him. If he had any idea I were female, he'd never have been so open. I can't believe I let it go this far... if I were in my human form, I'd be way past turned on right now.

I hear him shuffling around, followed by the sounds of a body splashing into the lake. I squint through my eyelids just enough to look at the pile of clothes he left behind, the black fabric of his boxers at the top of the heap.

He's completely naked.

In my lake.

I could join him. I could shift and follow him. He'd be shocked at first, but then he'd rise out of the water, wrap me in those powerful arms, and pull me down with him.

I have to leave.

GUESS MY BUDDY GOT BORED. I can't help but be a little disappointed at the wolf's absence when I return from the water. The clear morning air is still a bit chilly, and I hustle back into dry clothes as fast as my damp skin will allow.

The snap of branches brings an instant smile to my face, and I'm a little surprised at how happy I am to have my companion back.

"Hey, I need to find something to call you other than-"

It takes a second too long for my brain to catch up, as a freight train of snarling teeth and gold fur barrels toward me. I have just enough time to block, before fangs sink into my arm and the weight of the ambush sends me sprawling onto my back with my attacker in tow.

I don't have my weapons, but I'm far from defenseless. I punch him in the ear with my free hand, using the arm in his jaws to pull him close enough to bite the sensitive spot behind his nose. He yelps in surprise and pain, letting go just as my white wolf plows into his side, sending both tumbling.

I scramble for my Glock, but even before I have it in hand the wolves have separated. My wolf stands in front of me, tail and ears down, growling a warning. The gold wolf is a dozen paces away, between us and the water, mirroring my wolf's stance.

My hand is on my weapon where it's stowed inside my pack, but I don't move to pull it into view. I wait, braced to act if this escalates. I can assume the Shifters know each other, but whether that works in my favor or against it is yet to be seen.

The gold wolf shifts. The man that takes his place looks even more furious. He's wearing only a thin pair of pants and looks like a wild thing just as much in this form as his wolf.

"What is this?" He ignores my presence, directing his anger at the white wolf. "Is this where you've been? With a *human*?"

My wolf's growl drops an octave, his body in a crouch, ready to attack. Ready to defend.

The man takes a step back, his stance faltering as he shakes his head. His features twist as he presses his hands against his head.

"You better get your ass back." He growls the words through clenched teeth. "Because I swear, if you don't show yourself at the Meadow before noon, I'll be telling your... our Alpha... exactly where I found you."

Whatever weight that threat holds, he seems satisfied. He

shifts back to his wolf form, kicking up sand as he takes off for the forest.

"What the fuck?"

The white wolf turns, and those violet eyes are wide and bright. They snap to my arm, widening farther as a pitiful whine escapes him. I follow his gaze to my bloodied forearm, the shock and adrenaline making the wound painless.

"It's fine, I heal-"

Violet eyes hold mine as he shudders and contracts down into the form of a woman. My heart stops beating. Her hair is the palest blond, her features delicate. Her body is curved to perfection beneath ripped jeans and a sleeveless top.

Holy fuck. She's the most beautiful woman I've ever laid eyes on.

I'm dead. Or I'm delirious.

She grips my arm with firm confidence, my blood staining her flawless skin as she holds her small hands over the wounds.

"That bastard."

"It's okay. I have a Medic implant. I'll heal."

She looks at me with a desperate expression, her eyes searching mine. I reach out with my other hand, unable to resist touching her hair, her cheek, the gentle curve of her lower lip as it trembles under my thumb.

Fuck. I need to get away from this woman. This Shifter. If I don't, I'm going to do something stupid. Maybe it's the rush of the fight, but I'm really fucking close to kissing her. I've never felt this instantly drawn to a woman. She's not even human.

She's still looking at me, perfectly still as my hand refuses to stop touching her face. Those eyes. She's so delicate, so pure... my stomach turns at the thought. I pull my hand away, pushing up and away from her stare and her attentions.

What the fuck am I doing? Mercifully, the pain of the wolf's bite kicks in to distract me.

"I'll heal," I repeat, digging through my pack for first aid supplies.

I can't look at her when she crowds me again, swatting my hands as she takes over to wrap my arm with practiced skill. She's not the least bit concerned about the amount of my blood she has on her hands.

"Who are you?"

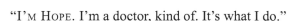

"I'M HOPE. I'm a doctor, kind of. It's what I do."

My fingers are shaking as I bind his arm. I'm always steady, but this man is... this whole situation has me feeling inside out. When Luke attacked and I thought he would kill him... the Presence, that hideous thing inside me, it flared to life stronger than I've ever felt it before.

If Luke hadn't backed off, I don't know what would have happened. He gripped his head like he was in pain. Could I have hurt him? Would this evil thing inside me make me turn against my own people?

I take a breath to steady myself, and my thoughts turn to the man in front of me. I should be worried about Luke and what he'll do when he gets back to the Meadow, but now all I can think about is the way this human looked at me. The way he touched my face like he could hardly believe I was real.

But it faded quickly enough. His reverent expression twisted into something closer to disgust as he pulled out of my grasp. Even now, when I finish securing the bandage on his arm, he doesn't waste a second before putting some distance between us.

The comfortable companionship we shared while I was in my wolf form is gone. I blink away the sting of that realization, then turn my back on him, heading for the lake to wash my hands.

"What's your name?"

"Gideon."

"You need to go, Gideon." His name feels strange on my tongue, but I think it suits him. I stand and shake off my hands before rubbing them dry on my jeans. "Luke will return with others."

"I can't go. Not until I get close enough to link with Tarek."

I spin on my heels. "Tarek?"

He stops in the midst of packing his gear, the white bandage on his arm already spotting red. When his eyes connect with mine, he looks away immediately. "Yeah. Tarek was my partner, my bonded Shifter, before Damon woke him up. Woke both of us up, really. Do you know him?"

Yeah, and I'll be knowing him a lot better soon. "I do."

Something flashes across his face, but it's gone as quickly as it came. "Get me close enough to link with him. I don't need to know exactly where the Meadow is, I just need to connect with him for five minutes, then I can go."

"Give me the message. Then you can go now. It'll be safer for you."

"Didn't sound like you were very welcome there, either."

"I have... obligations. I shouldn't have stayed out this long. Certainly not with a human, let alone a human like you."

"Why did you?" He sits on the ground, beads of sweat on his forehead despite the cool air. Resting his wounded arm on his backpack, he fishes out a small container and tips two white pills onto his hand. He might heal fast and be impervious to infection, but he's definitely feeling the pain.

"I don't know," I answer his question as I retrieve his water bottle and refill it at the lake. "I guess it was nice to talk with someone who didn't know who I was."

I hand him the water, and he looks from it to my eyes a few times before accepting it, as if the simple act of fetching him a drink is something strange.

"I did all the talking and... well, I might have acted a little differently if I'd known you weren't a male." A blush colors his cheeks, all the more obvious considering he's a little on the pale side at the moment.

"I didn't look." I instantly regret how juvenile that sounds. "I mean I... I gave you your privacy when you..."

He laughs, and judging by the heat that creeps up from my chest, I'm guessing I've turned a bright shade of red.

"How's the pain?" I ask, taking way too much effort to keep my voice professionally detached. If I could just stop replaying the slow-motion image of him undressing...

"Fine. It's fine." He shrugs a shoulder like it's no big deal, but I don't miss the way the shoulder attached to his injured arm stays held stiff. "You said you're a doctor?"

"Yes. At the Meadow I..." What am I doing? I shouldn't be telling him anything about the Meadow. How would I know what details could be twisted and used against us? "I can take your message to Tarek."

He shakes his head, pushing up to his feet. "I need to talk to him."

He continues packing his gear with one arm tucked against his side.

"I'm going back now. Even if you can track me, I'll be there long before you. I can take your message with me, or I can just tell them where you are and let the Alpha's decide what to do about you."

He stops what he's doing and faces me, his pale green eyes boring into mine. His expression is impossible to read, and I get the feeling that's not a good thing.

"Are you threatening me?"

I swallow past a lump in my throat. Crap, this man is intense. I spent the night and morning at his side, but I think this is the first time I'm meeting the Elite.

I don't break eye contact, but I brace myself, ready to shift and make a run for it if he comes at me.

After an uncomfortably long silence, his eyes drop to my mouth and then over to the lake. I let out the breath I was holding.

"The Elders suspect that the disappearing Shifters are developing a pack instinct, and that they're hiding out in Morwood." He goes back to packing the last of his gear. "They sent me to scout. When I tell them I found nothing, it won't deter them for long."

"Okay, what does that mean? If it's only suspicions and you aren't planning to tell them anything…"

"I don't assume the Elders are telling me everything. They tell me what they need me to know, so I'll do what they want me to do. Tarek will understand that, and the potential outcomes of returning with no useful intel."

"I'll tell him everything you said, and I'll tell the Alphas. If they come, we'll be ready."

He nods, his forehead creasing as he clenches and unclenches his jaw. He slings the heavy pack onto his back, but he doesn't make a move to go.

"Is there more?" It's obvious he's weighing a decision, but I can't guess about what.

He looks at me, his green eyes seeming a shade darker. His gaze rakes over me, the same way it did when he first saw my human form. I feel suddenly exposed, but also warm and tingly in all the right places.

Oh, blazes, why can't this man be a Shifter?

"What is it?" My voice sounds as breathless as I feel.

There's nothing wrong with being attracted to him. Any female would be insane not to melt under his stare. A few private fantasies won't harm anyone.

He walks a few paces closer. "I'm trying to decide if I'll regret leaving without asking to kiss you."

I gasp at his unexpected words, and he closes the distance between us. Threading the fingers of one hand through my hair, he leans in until the heat of his breath lingers with mine. I'm incapable of thought. The awareness of our bodies so close, the gentle caress of his thumb on my cheek...

"Or if kissing you only once would leave me with far greater regrets."

My heart has never beat this fast. My body has never felt this alive. The only thing I know for sure, is that if I don't grab on to this moment, I'll be the one who regrets it for the rest of my life.

I don't know how my lungs have enough air to speak, but I manage a whisper. "It's probably safer if you do."

He nods, his eyes focused on my mouth as his tongue slides out to moisten his lips. Lips I can kiss, if I just squeak out an ounce of courage.

"Can I kiss you, Hope?"

I rise onto my toes and press my mouth against his. I pull his full, soft lower lip between mine and shudder at the deep, sensual moan that rumbles in his chest. He tastes like lake, smoke, and desire.

We kiss like long-lost lovers who were never meant to be apart. We kiss like teenagers, drunk on the endless possibilities of life and love. We kiss like it's our first. Like it's our last. We melt into each other, into this moment we've stolen, as if we might choose to never return to the lives we left behind.

Then the moment's gone.

Cold air fills the space between us, chasing away the heat of his touch. I could cry, as the meaning of his words hits me.

Or if kissing you only once would leave me with far greater regrets.

I sink into my wolf form, tucking this memory safely away as I head back to face reality.

PRESENCE

"*A*re you that stupid, child?"

The venom in Mother's voice makes me back up a step. I assumed she would jump to warn the other Alphas about Gideon's message. That they would increase patrols and divert anyone working on the new cabins to speed up wall construction.

"No, Gideon-"

"Stop it." She waves her hand in front of her face, as if the mere mention of his name is an insult and a sign of my incompetence. "The humans send one of their soldiers with a message, and you automatically assume he's on our side? Please, spare me your ignorance for once."

I glance over at Luke, and he seems as shocked by my mother's reaction as I am. He got here first, of course, and filled her in on our confrontation at the lake. I'm sure he believed he was doing the right thing.

"We just need to speed up the wall-"

"Don't you understand? You were out there with a human. Alone. He could have... you need to understand that your safety, your future, means more than any of this."

"That's not true, Mother."

"Were you *with* him?"

Her question is so unexpected, I don't even know how to answer. I'm telling her the Elders are getting close to discovering our location, and she's more worried about me hooking up with a man she didn't choose.

"The safety of the Meadow-"

She steps toward me, her skin rippling at the edge of shifting. I haven't seen her take her wolf form in years.

Luke side-steps, coming closer to me as if he would defend me from my mother's temper.

"I won't let her out of my sight. She'll be safe."

"That was already your job!" She growls the words through clenched teeth.

"His job?" I look over at Luke, but his eyes are locked on Mother.

"Bring me Tarek." Mother's command has Luke jumping to obey. When he leaves us to do her bidding, she turns her dark eyes back to me. I don't bother telling her I delivered Gideon's message to Tarek first, and he's already waiting outside. "You will stay with Tarek, by his side, day and night. It's time for you to step up and do your part for the Meadow."

I try to keep calm, to let her have this rant without being baited into a fight, but the Presence is humming under my skin. It crawls through me, gripping my spine and climbing higher. I want to step back, give us both time to calm down and talk rationally... but the Presence wants to challenge, wants to fight.

Alpha.

I close my eyes, and for just a moment I let myself sink into the Darkness that's always waiting. As it surrounds my mind, anger consumes me.

"My part for the Meadow?" I growl the words, opening my eyes to lock with Mother's. "Everything I do is for the Meadow.

It's all I care about. Or do you mean my part to ensure you keep your place as Alpha, so you can use my life to keep your pathetic position of power?" I need to stop, but the anger is cathartic. The Presence is pooling at the base of my skull now and the pressure is almost painful. I swear I can see it reflected in Mother's eyes. "You'll never be a real Alpha. You're only here because Father risked everything to save you."

"Grow up, child."

The Presence digs its claws in behind my eyes, just as fiercely as it did back at the lake. And just like Luke, Mother's features are twisting, her jaw clenching, her slender fingers digging into her palms.

I step closer. She stumbles as she growls through clenched teeth. "Life isn't a love story and you have no idea the depth of-"

"Silence!" My father's voice explodes in the room. He stands, taller than I've ever seen him as he subdues Mother with a single command. I've never heard him speak to her like that.

"Father..."

"You don't need to understand this, Hope."

I don't recognize the man that commands me with cold, emotionless eyes, and I shrink beneath his gaze.

"You need to trust us. Go with Tarek and do as you are told."

The Presence has retreated fully. It's never backed away from even the hint of a confrontation, but Father's sudden dominance sent it running. I look away from the stranger in his body, to my mother whose eyes are lowered in the first display of submission I've ever seen from her.

Trust them? I don't think I know them.

I don't even know myself.

"What's happening?" My voice cracks beneath the weight of this moment that I can barely make sense of.

The silence stretches on, but I wait.

Mother shifts and her slim, black-furred wolf lopes out of the tent. I turn to Father, but his face is a mask.

They know. They felt the Presence and saw it in my eyes. They know something's wrong with me. Are they scared of me now? Disappointed in me? What would have happened if Father hadn't interrupted? I've never felt such anger, such a need to dominate... and it felt so good.

I turn and leave the way I came.

Outside in the noon sun, Tarek waits. His thick arms are crossed, his brow furrowed. As big as he is; a wall of muscle containing the power of a dragon... could this thing inside me bring him to his knees?

"Do you not see how wrong this is?" I say as I walk past him, denying the urge to shift as he matches my pace with ease.

"I am loyal to the Meadow."

I know he is. I can sense it in him, unwavering and steady. He would protect this place with fists and talons, or even mate the Alpha's daughter if asked.

"So am I."

Am I loyal enough to do what's best for them? To chase away any threat, even if that threat is me? The good I do at the clinic... does it outweigh the evil inside me?

"The Meadow is the Shifters. It's the people that call it home." Tarek's words make me stop to look at his face. "Anyone who isn't thinking about the best interests of the people doesn't deserve the loyalty of the Meadow."

His expression is hard; determined. The loyalty I sensed in him was never for my mother. Something heavy settles in my gut as a group of Shifters pass us on the path. When they're out of earshot, Tarek leans down close to my ear.

"I'm going to find Gideon and help him get out of

Morwood before someone gets the bright idea to hunt him down."

Would Mother go that far? She was furious at me for being alone with him. Like my being with someone other than the mate she chose would be such a terrible thing. Like her plan to keep her position could matter more than the very safety of the Meadow.

"He's injured. His arm."

Tarek nods, then walks with long strides that make me have to jog to keep up.

"You'll have to come with me, if you plan to obey your mother."

Obey her? After what happened back there, I'm well past disobeying. And if this thing is still gaining strength inside me, if it feeds off my anger and has the ability to hurt others... how can I risk being near the people I care about?

YOU SHOULD GO

*T*arek holds out a hand, and I grab it gratefully as he pulls me to my feet. I glance around to see if Gideon saw my ungraceful decent from the saddle, but the small clearing is empty.

"Is he close?"

"He passed this spot recently. He's backtracking to meet us here."

No sooner does he say the words, and I hear the crack of a dead branch. Gideon pushes through the trees, and my temperature spikes as my mind returns to the lake; to when he peeled off his clothing for a swim, and when we kissed like all of eternity had existed solely for that one moment.

He spots me and his expression is neither warm, nor cold. Only his eyes register a hint of surprise. I attempt a casual smile, but it feels awkward, so I look away.

"You didn't tell me you had a passenger."

"Good to see you, too, G."

Gideon strides up to Tarek, who stands half a foot taller and carries about fifty extra pounds of pure muscle on his thick frame. He slaps him on the shoulder, but I can feel his eyes haven't left me.

"It's good to see you, Tarek."

"You've already met Hope, my mate."

I nearly choke as my eyes snap to Gideon. "I'm not his mate." I look at Tarek, worried that I'll offend him. It's the first time he's said that out loud. "Not yet, I mean, I..."

Tarek laughs, putting a heavy hand on my shoulder. I bite my tongue before I dig myself a deeper hole. What does it matter if Gideon thinks we're mated?

"Hope's mother is the leader of their Alpha's." Tarek explains, and I lower my eyes, wondering what the point of this is.

"Is that so?"

"Yep. And Molly has decided that the best way to make sure she keeps that position is by having her only daughter mated to a dragon Shifter."

Gideon's only response is a huff that sounds a lot like disapproval. I peek up at him, more than a little mortified at this entire conversation.

"And what do you say about that, Hope? Do you want to..." he clears his throat, "... *mate* Tarek?"

Heat rises in my cheeks. "I... If it's best-"

"-for the Meadow." Tarek finishes my sentence with a laugh, and my embarrassment turns to anger as the Presence starts its climb.

"Don't think for a second that you understand our history! You just got here, and you think you know better than the people who started everything?" I feel guilty for my outburst, but I cross my arms and lean into it. "I'm a doctor. I've served the medical needs of my people since before you were born. Mating with you won't be the most unpleasant procedure I've performed, nor the least."

The shock on Tarek's face is immediate and satisfying. I can hear Gideon laughing through the temper roaring in my ears, but I don't look his way.

"I might be new, but I recognize a leader who cares more ab-"

"Easy, Tarek." Gideon interrupts. "Just take me to Moridian. Then you two can fight like an old married couple all you want."

I turn to Gideon, ready to give him a piece of my mind, but his expression doesn't match the tone of his voice. His eyes are tired; sad even.

I close my mouth, conceding to let his comment slide.

He looks like he might say something, but instead he reaches toward my face, his thumb brushing over my lower lip like he did when I first shifted in front of him.

I'm frozen to the spot. I can't pull away from his gaze that seems to be melting from sadness into something much warmer. With my heart beating erratically, I reach up and place my hand over his.

"You should go with him." Tarek's voice shatters the moment, whatever it was, and Gideon and I both take a step back.

"What? No..."

"Why not? Why go back and be used as someone else's puppet?"

I want to argue with him. I want to tell him I'm needed. I can't just walk away from everyone I care about… but I recall my mother's face as the Presence fed off my anger and caused her physical pain. I'm a healer, but I hurt people.

"Brom can handle the clinic," Tarek says. "The whole point of the Meadow is to stop Shifters from being used by people whose agendas are more important than our lives. Why should you have to live that way?"

"She can't come with me." Gideon speaks up, and even though I might agree with him, his words still sting. "If I show up with a Shifter, it won't go unnoticed."

"No one will know she's a Shifter."

He laughs, running a hand through his hair. "If I show up with a woman, it'll raise even more red flags."

"She'll be safer with you."

"No, she won't."

Tarek growls. "Fine. You can leave her with Kelsey."

Now it's Gideon's turn to growl, though it's hardly as effective coming from his human chest.

"Mother would be furious with you," I say, but what's the alternative? What am I returning to if I go back to the Meadow now? If they finally realize what I've always tried to hide; that I'm defective. Maybe even dangerous.

And yeah, what about freedom? The Meadow represents freedom for Shifters, so why don't I get to be free? I'm ashamed of the selfish thought, but even the Presence reacts to the idea. I am free. I choose to stay, I choose to work at the clinic, and I choose to mate Tarek to secure my Mother's position.

I can also choose to leave.

"I'll tell her you ran," Tarek says, not giving up his argument. "Not my fault. What's the worst she can do? Maybe she'll show her true colors and get booted off that imaginary throne of hers."

"She might tell you to leave the Meadow."

"That's fine. I'll earn her good favor back by hunting you down and taking you straight to my bed." I snap my eyes to his, and he raises his hands in surrender.

"Fuck, Tarek." Gideon scrubs both hands through his hair as he turns and walks a few paces away. With his arms above his head that way, a sliver of skin is revealed between his shirt and the top of his pants. "I won't help you piss off the fucking Shifter Alpha by kidnapping her daughter."

"It's not kidnapping. I want to go." I can't believe I said that out loud.

Gideon turns, his pale eyes burning into mine as if he means to read my thoughts.

Tarek claps his hands together. "Don't let me talk you into anything. I don't mind the idea of making you-"

"Have you ever been to Moridian?" Gideon asks, blatantly ignoring Tarek. "Or to any human city?"

"Yes. On supply runs. Sometimes we stay for a few days to gather everything we need."

Mother thought it was important that I experience human culture and understand their technology, so I wouldn't be overwhelmed if we were ever forced to live in the city.

Luke was always with me on those runs, keeping me from exploring like I wanted to. I thought it was just him being him, but after what Mother said today, I'm not so sure. He may have always been her eyes and ears, staying close so I couldn't get too close to anyone else.

I look over at Tarek, and despite the teasing, his eyes are serious.

"I've heard about Kelsey." My words sound more confident than I feel. "I could stay there. Just for a little while."

The corner of Tarek's mouth twitches as he restrains a smile.

"Will you tell Damon for me?" It's better if Tarek's the one to tell him I'm gone. Then he'll think that I'm running off to claim my freedom and enjoy a little rebellion before I commit. I won't have to lie to him or see the look in his eyes if I tell him the real reason I'm leaving.

Tarek nods, his smile breaking free.

Gideon doesn't look happy, but he seems to have resigned himself to the fact that this is happening.

I'm leaving the Meadow.

BABYSITTER

"Come on, Kelsey. You're killing me here."

"I'm sorry, Gideon. I'm happy to provide a safe, private place for Shifters to relax and have a drink. But I'm no babysitter."

"Neither am I!"

She laughs, patting my chest as she shakes her head. "You're the one who brought a souvenir back from the forest. She's your responsibility."

I look over my shoulder. Hope is still sitting in the booth I deposited her in, her eyes as big as saucers as she takes in everything and everyone around her. She looks so vulnerable. So innocent.

"I don't want to hurt her."

Kelsey chokes on her drink. "I think she's more likely to hurt you, big guy. She might look delicate now, but I'm betting she could tear you a new one if you earned an ass kicking."

"Fuck, Kelsey. You're killing me."

"Yes, you said that already."

Goddamnit, if I'd had any clue I'd end up bringing her back with me, I'd never have kissed her. It was a stupid move. I've never been that drawn to someone. That desperate to connect; to taste. A little guilty pleasure and a sweet memory to keep.

I never intended to lead her on or make her think I had anything more to offer.

She knew that. I know she did. We kissed like lovers, and the moment it was over she shifted and left. She recognized that it wasn't a beginning, it was an ending. It wasn't anything at all, really, just a whim and an opportunity too sweet to pass up.

I can't take her home. She's too much. The afternoon spent pressed against her in Tarek's saddle was torture enough.

"If I take a woman like her home, it'll just draw attention. Especially after the Horizon Zero shit."

"Pretend she's your girlfriend. Your buddies will be happy to see you in the game again, and no one will suspect she's a Shifter. Plus, you're always turning the ladies down, having a decoy girlfriend will get them off your back."

"I can be a decoy girlfriend." I nearly jump out of my skin at Hope's sudden appearance at my side. "If it helps keep you out of trouble."

Fuck, no. There's no way I'm pretending to be anything with her. The forest, the lake, it made me sentimental and soft. But I'm no safe shelter for her.

"You don't want to stay with me, Hope. I live up on the Solar. You'd be stuck in my flat while I'm at work, with nowhere to go and no way to get back to Morwood."

Her eyes drop to the floor as she chews on her lower lip. There's no way she wants to be trapped up there. An arranged marriage has to be a far better option than being stuck in a prison of metal and air.

"It's just for a little while. I'll pretend... I won't get you into trouble."

"Perfect," Kelsey adds, putting a hand on Hope's arm. "Problem solved."

Fuck. Now the two of them are teamed up. It's not the trouble I'll be in that worries me. Hell, I'm this close to packing up and leaving all this Protector bullshit in my dust as it is. She won't be safe in a city of humans. She certainly won't be safe under my roof.

"Kelsey..."

"Final answer, handsome. And it's nothing personal, Hope. You're welcome to spend as much time here as you like during business hours, but I can't get all this mixed up with my personal life."

"It's okay. I understand."

Hope's looking up at me with those violet eyes of hers. Fuck, why did I have to kiss her? Wondering what it would be like was far easier than knowing and not being able to go back for more.

"Your truck's still parked out back," Kelsey says.

I could walk away. These women hold no control over me, and I could easily walk away from this. Hope can fend for herself. Find her own way home. But even as I consider doing just that, a selfish thought settles in the back of my mind.

Her company back at the lake was a welcome change from my usual solitude. I assumed she was a male at first, but still. The chance to have a few more nights around that campfire sounds damn appealing.

She watches me and waits for my final answer, her teeth working nervously at the soft flesh of her lip.

"Let's go." I turn away so I don't have to see relief or gratitude on her face. I'm being a selfish prick right now, because I know damn well that taking her home is a bad idea.

Hope keeps close as I lead her through the back room and out into the late afternoon haze. When I open the passenger door of my truck, she stays planted. Shit, I hadn't even considered how new this would all be for her.

"Have you ever been in a vehicle?"

"Yes." Her eyes scan the lot and the other vehicles until they land on the bar's back entrance. Her pink tongue darts out to moisten her lips.

"You're smart to be having second thoughts." Her eyes find mine and widen as her chest expands with a deep breath. "You don't really know me. I can take you back to Morwood."

"No." She shakes her head fiercely, as if she might shake away all her doubts. "No, I can't. I just... I thought I'd be staying with Kelsey."

A nagging thought pulls at me. The same one I had when she first stated she wanted to come here; there's more going on than she's admitting.

Running away from an arranged marriage, fine, I don't blame her for wanting out of that situation. But she's a doctor at the Meadow, a natural Shifter, daughter of one of the Alpha's... seems to me someone like her would stand up for what they want, not walk away from everything and everyone they know.

It was one thing to be staying with Kelsey, in a location close enough that she could make her way back to the forest whenever she chose. A couple days away to think it all through.

Coming with me is another story entirely. She'll be stuck with nowhere to go but my small flat. No way to get home without me taking her. You don't commit to something like that unless you aren't planning to go home anytime soon.

What's she really running from?

I wait, holding the door and keeping my mouth shut.

She looks at my truck, then at me. She smiles. I hold out my hand, as if she would need any help. She takes it anyway, if only to humor me.

I drive in silence as she watches Moridian pass by, her eyes reflecting the city lights. Dusk comes early down here, under the blanket of pollution. I open my window when we pull into the toll booth, then swipe my comm.

"This is the teleport," I warn her as we roll into the dock that resembles a shipping container. "It's going to feel a little weird, but it won't last long."

I hope I'm telling her the truth. I hardly notice a buzz anymore, but for some it's far more unpleasant. None of this tech is from Earth, and Terrans all seem to react differently to it. Not that Shifters are technically Terrans...

She clutches the seat, her spine rigid as she looks at me with wide eyes.

"It's fine. Perfectly normal." I grit my teeth, hating that she's uncomfortable.

In a few moments, the wall in front of us opens, and I pull out into the glow of Solar One. Hope gasps. I don't know if she understands that we've just teleported to thirty thousand feet above sea level, but she's already so overwhelmed with it all I don't want to overload her.

"It's beautiful." Her voice is reverent, with no trace of the discomfort she felt in the teleport.

I release my white-knuckled grip on the steering wheel. "Not half as beautiful as your lake."

I've always lived on Solar One. My father was an Elite before he retired. My mother's the daughter of a High Judge. This is all I've ever known.

My life could have gone one of two ways; law school or the Academy. It was an easy choice. But the forest is where I feel most alive; most like myself. Living off the land. Sleeping under the unfiltered stars. I suppose it's just human nature to feel like the grass is greener on the other side. Being born into privilege and raised with wealth and technology makes it easy to taste the simpler side of life and think it's sweeter.

Hope puts a hand against the window as she looks through

the glass at the towering, metallic buildings of the city. She catches me watching and folds her hands in her lap. I'm making her uncomfortable, but fuck, I can't stop looking at her. Her open fascination is beautiful.

I drive a meandering path so she can look her fill. I point out places of interest now and then, but mostly we drive in silence.

The sky is dark when I park at my building, the clouds blocking most of the stars. I hesitate to get out. The valet is waiting patiently, but the longer I delay, the more out of place it looks.

"Is everything okay?"

"I'll get your door."

DECOY

*G*ideon opens my door and holds out a hand. I reach to take it, but I can't seem to move that last inch. He made the same gesture when I got into the truck, and the warmth of his big, rough palm was far more enjoyable than it should have been. I grab the door instead and hop to the ground.

Gideon passes something to a young man, then gestures for me to follow him toward the looming, metal building. Seeing the city through the windows of the truck is nothing compared to being here, staring up at the vast towers of metal and lights.

I knew Solar One would be different from Moridian, but it looks like another planet entirely. I want to go to the edge and look down at the ground city and Morwood. I've never been higher than the peak of North Mountain.

I jump when Gideon's hand grazes my back, guiding me to follow him toward the building. Stop staring like a tourist, Hope. Stop acting like it's your first time on the Solar. I'm supposed to be passing as his girlfriend, and I'm sure someone like him wouldn't be dating a sightseeing hitchhiker.

An older male opens the door and gives me a smile, but his

brow is furrowed. Gideon mumbles a quick greeting as he hurries us through.

The space inside is brilliant. Everything is white and gold, with lights like the noon sun glaring down from the ceiling. I touch the leaf of a lush fern that's growing in a little oasis, then jerk my hand away at the waxy chill of stiff plastic between my fingers.

My stomach lurches as I wonder for the first time if anything green actually grows up here. It should have been obvious, but the sudden realization that I'm so far from nature gives me a hard rush of cold feet about this whole situation.

I clutch Gideon's arm, relieved when he doesn't pull away. The connection to something living steadies me. I lean into him, breathing deep and appreciating the lingering scent of the forest on his clothes.

A woman behind a polished desk nods as we pass, her eyes giving me an obvious once-over. I grip Gideon's arm tighter as I offer a smile she doesn't return.

"Why are they all looking at me that way?"

"It's late. I don't…" He looks down at me, pressing his lips into a thin line. "I don't bring women home. I told you it would be suspicious."

He'd said that, but I assumed he was only trying to talk me out of coming. If my presence alone draws attention, and someone guesses what I am… I can't let my problems cost Gideon his job. Or worse.

"Don't act so stiff. Put your arm around me, at least."

He looks down at me like I've said something absurd. Since the moment Tarek suggested I come here with him, Gideons only looked at me with that chill in his eyes. Whatever heat passed between us at the lake is long gone.

Maybe he regrets it. Maybe he only wanted to see what it would be like to kiss a Shifter. Maybe I was the only one who felt the earth move, and he was just crossing something off his bucket list.

It doesn't matter. I'm here now, and for both our sakes, this has to look real.

I summon my courage, scooting tight against him to wrap my arm around his waist. He sucks in a breath, and the muscles in his abdomen turn rock hard. I ignore the heat that flares in my belly and spreads through my body.

It's no different than it was with Damon. A little platonic touching and everyone gets the message. It's nothing to get all hot and bothered by.

"Settling in for the night with a guest, Sir?" A man with white gloves pushes a tiny button on the wall as he looks from me to Gideon and back.

"Yes. Thank you."

The doors slide open to reveal a small, square lift. I whisper to Gideon as we step inside, "You could at least act like you're not disgusted by me."

I shouldn't have said that. It doesn't matter if he regrets the kiss or not. He was perfectly clear that he doesn't want me here. I'm the one who needs a place to hide out. I'm the one who convinced him to bring me along.

I jump when he puts his hand on my hip. He leans down, and I shudder when his breath ghosts across my ear. "Why would you think I'm disgusted by you?"

"It's obvious. And it's fine, really. But you're worried about this looking suspicious-"

He releases my hip as he turns to face me, blocking my view as the doors slide closed. His hand grazes the side of my neck, and I close my eyes as a shiver passes through me.

He's just taking my advice and putting on a show, but his touch still feels far better than it should. His thumb brushes lightly across my cheek, and I keep my eyes closed tight as he tilts my head.

His lips brush against mine so softly, it could be my imagination. I suck in a breath that floods my senses with him, and the lift starts to rise.

"They have security cameras here and in the hall." He speaks in barely more than a whisper, his mouth still brushing mine. "Would this be less suspicious?"

Then he's kissing me.

I'm frozen in place as his mouth presses against mine. It's so unexpected, I don't know what to do. I'm just standing here, lost.

He pulls away, still close enough that he's all I can see, all I can smell. I want to kiss him back. I want to... I don't know what I'm thinking.

"Put your arms around my neck."

I do as he says, my limbs shaking as I thread my arms around him. With one wide hand against the small of my back, he pulls me tight against a solid wall of muscle and strength.

"Kiss me."

I can't breathe. The raw edge in his voice feels too real.

I obey. With my arms around his neck, I press my mouth against his. Just like at the lake, I pull his lower lip between mine. When he inhales with a shudder, it echoes over my entire body.

A growl rumbles in my chest, and I tighten my grip around his neck as his fingers thread through my hair. The kiss deepens, our tongues clashing as exploration becomes something needy.

The lift doors open and he pulls away, grabbing my hand to lead me out into a bright hallway.

I don't know what to feel after that kiss. He was only trying to fool the cameras, but my entire body's vibrating. All the emotions that consumed me at the lake are back in full force.

He opens a door, pulls me through, and pushes me back against the wall. I'm hardly breathing as he braces his arms on either side of my head. Pale light washes through wide windows, casting his face in shadow as he leans in until his breath mingles with mine again.

Then I do the stupidest thing I've ever done.

"Are they still watching us here?"

He pauses, draws a deep breath, and steps away.

I want to grab his shirt and pull him close again. I step toward him, but he takes an equal step back.

"No. Not here. I'm... sorry."

He turns his back to me, moving to turn on lights and chase away the last remnants of whatever that was. That's the second time he's kissed me and regretted it. I'd be furious if it didn't hurt so much.

What am I thinking? I'm not here to play or experiment. I'm not here for a fun vacation or a romantic fling with a human. I'm here because I have nowhere else to go; because I need to find out what I am and what to do about it.

I pull my eyes away from Gideon as I look around the place I'll be calling home for the moment. It's a wide sitting area that turns into a kitchen beyond. Everything's white and tidy, and there's nothing that reminds me of the man I met hiking through the forest.

He moves around the space, unpacking his backpack. I watch him for a while, but he doesn't even glance my way.

There's a set of patio doors to the left of the kitchen, leading out onto a big balcony. Two other doors on the opposite wall are partially closed, blocking my view inside.

On my few trips to Moridian, we stayed in cheap motels and kept our heads down. This flat is nothing like those places.

I push off from the wall, keeping my eyes away from Gideon as I explore the space.

I peek inside one of the other doors to see a bedroom that's as stark and impersonal as the rest. The other opens into a small bathroom.

"You can have the bedroom."

Gideon's voice is casual. When I hazard a glance at him, his expression is neutral. It's like nothing even happened for him, yet I'm wired like I ate a pound of sugar. I take a deep breath, then a few more, and tell myself I'm just as unaffected as he is.

"Your flat isn't at all like I imagined."

"Oh? What did you expect?"

"I'm not sure. You seemed much more at home in the forest."

He nods, a half smile softening his features.

"I'm not disgusted by you, Hope. Far from it. It would just be better if I were."

My mouth goes dry. Why is he affecting me so much? It was just a kiss. Two kisses. And he's a human... not that there's anything wrong with that, but...

"Why? Why would it be better?"

The expression that washes over his face makes my heart ache. I want to ask him what it means, but he changes the subject. "I'll report to HQ tomorrow. Tell them I came up empty-handed."

"What happens then?"

"They'll find the Meadow, eventually. But with Damon and Tarek on duty, they won't have an easy time getting close."

"I'm not abandoning the Meadow. I just need a little time. A few days."

I hate that he might think I'm running away just to shirk my duties. I want him to know there's more to it, but I can't tell him the truth. I wouldn't even know how to start if I tried.

He's looking at me with narrowed eyes and a clenched jaw. I can't stop my eyes from dropping to his mouth.

"Nothing will happen in the next few days. Probably much longer. You can take time to figure your shit out, and the only thing it will hurt is your mother's pride."

I close my eyes. I've already hurt far more than just her pride.

"It's late. Get some sleep. You can worry about it in the morning."

CAMILLA

$\mathcal{I}$ can't sleep.

The sounds are all wrong. The big bed is soft and warm, but I push away the covers and slide off, pausing for a moment to knead my toes into the plush carpeting. I'd sleep easier in my wolf form, but it doesn't seem right in this place. And I wouldn't want to shed on Gideon's bed.

But it's more than just that. I can't just sit here and hope the mere passing of time will give me answers.

I grab my jeans off the floor, pulling them on along with my shirt. I tip-toe quietly across the room.

I peek through a crack in the door, into the main room that's bathed in silver light. Gideon's on the sofa, his body covered by a blanket. His face is hidden from this angle. I watch him for a moment, until I'm confident his steady breathing means he's asleep. Then I creep quietly to the bathroom.

The bedroom doesn't hold any of his scent, not even the bed itself, but this room smells distinctly masculine. I reach out and touch a plush, white towel hanging beside the tub, brushing my thumb over a small, beige embroidered *gg*.

I heard him showering in here after I closed myself in the

bedroom. That mental image was almost as much torture as when he was naked in my lake.

I shamelessly inhale the soapy, clean scent. Something rich and spicy wafts from the cupboard beside the sink. Gideon smells like the forest, and male sweat, and the lake... but I suppose he doesn't always smell that way.

I open the cupboard just to satisfy my curiosity. An amber bottle is the source of the pleasantly spicy scent, but that's not what grabs my attention now. There's a hairbrush with a few long strands still entwined in its bristles. Two toothbrushes. A small, pale blue deodorant stick beside a larger gray one.

I close the cupboard.

It doesn't matter that he has a mate. Why would it? It would be silly to think a man like him wouldn't have someone.

The suspicious looks from the people downstairs...

I cover my face with my hands. Oh, blazes. They were looking at me that way because they thought he was cheating on her. And that performance we put on in the elevator... how could I have been so naive?

I push out of the bathroom, hurrying past Gideon's sleeping form as fast as I can without waking him. It takes a few tries for me to figure out the latch on the sliding balcony door, but then the heat of embarrassment fades as I breathe in the cool night air. It smells like metal and humans.

I grip the iron railing as I stare down at the streets that are impossibly far below. The moon is hidden behind thick clouds. The silver lighting the sky seems to be the glow of the city itself.

How can I find any answers in a place like this? I close my eyes, blocking out my artificial surroundings. But there's no peace behind my eyelids. The Darkness is immense, the Presence waiting, beckoning. What would happen if I let it take me?

The patio doors squeak, pulling me out of the Darkness with

a jolt. I don't turn around. My heart races as Gideon's thick, bare arms come into view. He leans on the railing beside me, close enough that the heat of his body warms me.

His cargo pants are replaced by loose sweats and a sleeveless, white shirt clinging tightly to his torso. A fresh bandage wraps his arm where Luke bit him, tied in the awkward way that results from using one hand and teeth.

"Can't sleep?" His eyes lock with mine, the pale green iris's lit with the glow of the Solar.

What would he do if I kissed him? Would he kiss me back? Would he press me against the railing and let me feel every hard inch of him against me, or would he pull me back to the bed that's plenty big enough for two...

Such pointless thoughts, and yet I can't help my mind from going there. I suppose it's logical. He's so far removed from everything I've known; the opposite of the mate I thought I was waiting for. It's only natural that the temptation he poses would be appealing on some juvenile level.

And then there's that other detail...

"You have a mate."

His brow furrows, as if the accusation confuses him.

"I saw her things in your bathroom. I thought... it's fine, of course. I just..." I close my eyes. Why am I even bringing this up?

I jump when he touches my face. He's looking down at me with the hint of a smile and a little too much heat in his eyes. I should back away. This isn't fair to the woman who's earned shelf space in his bathroom, even if she hasn't earned his loyalty.

"You embarrass easily," he says, as his thumb brushes back and forth over my cheek. "Your cheeks turn pink, and you bite your lower lip."

His thumb moves to stroke across my mouth, and by sheer

force of will I take a big step back. His eyes widen just slightly, but his smile deepens. He goes back to leaning on the railing, his eyes focused down at the streets below.

"Camilla."

He says the name with obvious affection. The single word says more than enough, and I turn to go back inside.

"She was my niece." His confession makes me pause, but it's the hitch of pain in his tone that has me turning back. "She stayed here after Whisper got her out. She lived here until she..."

His head dips, hanging off his shoulders as he leans on the railing, his hands scrubbing through his hair. Tears sting behind my eyes as I put two-and-two together, remembering the story of the girl Whisper saved. The niece of an Elite, who was abducted after the suspected murder of her mother.

Gideon's niece. Gideon's sister.

"I'm so sorry."

I put my hand on his back, but he tips his face away. I kiss his shoulder, letting my mouth linger on smooth skin over thick, taut muscle. He's in pain. He's lost so much.

He's not mated.

Whatever the future holds for me, I'm here now, in this place with this man. We could both use a moment to feel alive in the middle of the twisted hand fate has dealt us.

I slide my hand down his back and under the hem of his shirt. His bare skin is hot against my palm. I summon my courage even though my insides are trembling, and I flick out my tongue to taste the salty skin of his shoulder.

With that incredible speed, his hands are cupping my face and he's kissing me like he would devour me if he could. He pushes me back against the railing, and a moan is ripped from my chest as his arousal presses into my stomach.

His kiss is relentless; starving. I wrap my arms around his

neck to grab fistfuls of his hair as I kiss him back with an intensity I didn't know I was capable of.

He pulls away, leaving me breathless as he retreats until his back hits the door, his chest heaving as his arousal tents the front of his sweats. I can't tear my eyes off him. Standing there like that, he's the vision of pure, masculine beauty.

And he wants me, even though he's fighting it. Maybe it's because I'm a Shifter, or maybe because of the situation with Tarek. I don't know what's making him hold back, but I sure as hell want him to stop.

I step toward him, but before I can touch him the expression on his face stops me. It's sorrow, and frustration, and fear. Oh, no. He's grieving the loss of his family, and I twisted it into something sexual. He needed comfort, and I threw myself at him like it was irrelevant.

I reach out, slowly, and rest my hand over his heart. It's beating as fiercely as mine. He doesn't stop me when I close the distance between us, fitting my body to his as I wrap my arms around his waist and rest my head on his chest. As much as it lights my blood on fire, I ignore the press of his arousal, fighting the urge to move my hips and get better acquainted.

After a few moments, he relaxes and his great arms wrap around me. He strokes my hair with his chin resting gently on my head, and I listen as his heartbeat slows and his body softens. It's the most intimate moment I've ever shared with another soul.

"Where the hell did you come from, Hope?"

His voice is thick and low, and I smile as he presses a kiss to the top of my head.

COMMON EMOTION

"*F*uck!"

I should have left the bandage on until after I cooked the bacon.

Hope's laughter brings an automatic smile to my face, and I look over to see her emerging from my bedroom. She's wearing the same jeans and t-shirt, though she must have shifted because they look crisp and freshly washed. Her pale hair is tied back, and those violet eyes are dancing.

But it's her mouth that commands my attention.

I forget about the bacon sizzling on the stove, as I recall what it felt like to kiss her. The sensual exploration at the lake. The uncertain heat in the elevator. And just after midnight last night... The raw passion that erupted out of her small body. The strength in her arms as she pulled me closer. How fucking amazing would it be to lay her down, to feel her surrounding me and watch her face as she detonates.

I've kissed this woman three times, and each time I fall a little deeper. Not love, no, but lust like I've never felt before. I need to rein it in. I have more self-control than this.

But fuck, I've never been so tempted to just throw caution

to the wind. I knew it was a bad idea to bring her here. It's too much, too close. Seeing her in my home. In my bed. It's making my self-control bend, and she deserves better than that. She deserves to know who she's getting involved with.

"Bacon giving you trouble?"

She grabs my hand, and I can't think about anything but her touch as she inspects the new skin that marks where her friend took a piece of me.

I jump as another stinging splash from the pan nails me, and her delicious laugh makes me instantly hungry for something sweeter than fried meat.

I force that thought away as I turn my attention back to the stove, and dish up two plates of steaming eggs and bacon. She thanks me as she accepts her share, a faint blush creeping up her cheeks.

As fiery as this woman can be, she sure embarrasses easily.

We sit at the table and eat in comfortable silence, as I try not to let her catch me watching her. She fascinates me. Everything about her.

When Damon first let it slip that he was sleeping with Whisper, I thought it was a bit of a gray area at best... full out bestiality at worse. But Tarek and Damon aren't animals and Hope isn't anything less than a woman.

Hell, she's a better person than most I've met.

In the brief time I've known her, she's defended a stranger without concern for her own safety, accepted the fate dealt to her simply because it was best for her people, and risked everything to strike out on her own. I've seen her surge with passion and melt with compassion.

Have I really only known her for a few days?

When she finishes her plate, I stand and take her dishes. She follows me to the sink and sets to washing while I dry.

It's comfortable. Too comfortable.

Even with Lily, it wasn't like this. There was never any peace through her anger. Everything was a test. Nothing was ever enough. But I deserved it. I deserved all her resentment; all her hate.

I sure as hell don't deserve to be standing here happily washing dishes with another woman.

I finish as quick as I can, but when I turn to leave the kitchen, Hope's soft hand wraps around my wrist, her skin warm and damp from the dishwater.

"Are you okay?"

I look into those stunning eyes, and for the first time I'm compelled to talk about it. Like I could explain everything. Tell her what I did. Would she react as she did when she dressed my arm; not even blinking at the ruined flesh and the blood running over her skilled hands? Would she do the smart thing and walk away?

I have to touch her. I run my thumb across her cheek, soaking up the heat that flares in her eyes as her lips part on a sigh.

"You deserve someone who will love you without reservation. Without baggage and bullshit."

She snorts as she rolls her eyes, pushing my hand from her face.

"I'm done waiting for love."

I feel my eyebrows raise as I force myself to keep a straight face. I cross my arms over my chest, waiting for her to continue. There's a rant bubbling under the surface, her lips twitching as she fights the urge to let it out.

"My whole life, I believed I was waiting for *the one*. The perfect mate who would just walk into my world, and I'd know it was him the moment I spotted him. I never doubted that for a second. But it wasn't real. It was never going to happen that way. Mother was filling my head with childish fantasies to keep me waiting until she found the one *she* wanted for me."

Her cheeks flush pink when she pauses, and she shoves her hands in her pockets as she chews her lip. It's none of my business, but I can't resist asking...

"You waited? Do you mean-"

"No!" She blushes a deeper shade, then lowers her voice, "No. I'm not... I didn't... I mean I waited for love. I held out for that strike of lightening, instead of letting myself enjoy the moments, you know?"

Not a virgin, then. Something too much like jealousy rises in my chest, and I tamp it down just as fast. Her sex life, past or present, is none of my fucking concern.

"I'm not sure it matters either way." I put some distance between us, retrieving my keys and jacket. "Whether it's a moment or a lifetime commitment, it's all just hormones and circumstance."

Why the fuck did I just say that? She doesn't need to hear my jaded opinions.

"Are you saying you've never been in love?"

I walked right into that one. For some stupid reason, I glance over at her. She's looking at me with such sadness you'd think I just told her my dog died. I shrug my jacket on over my shoulders, and I can hear her following close behind me as I head for the door.

"It's not a real thing, Hope. Love is a common emotion, but the concept of being in love with one other person is just a temporary state of mind. Stay put while I'm gone, okay? It's not safe for you to leave without me."

"I know plenty of couples who are in love. Whisper and Damon..."

I turn and brush my thumb across her cheek. That's all it takes to shut her up, her lips parting as she sucks in a breath.

"There's no such thing as happily ever after. There's only happy for now."

It's an attempt to warn her away, and I can't for the life of me understand why those words bring a wide smile to her face. I can't help myself. I lean down and press a brief kiss to her forehead.

It takes all my strength to pull away from her, and I allow myself the pleasure of trailing my fingers down her soft neck and along the edge of her shirt. Fuck, I want to follow that trail with my tongue.

I step back until she's out of reach, not at all disappointed to see her breathing like she just ran a mile.

"Happy for now sounds pretty good, Gideon."

SKYE

A long, warm shower with all the vivid, hot Gideon fantasies I've been saving up... yes, please. It's a delicious luxury. Alone in his flat, I'm not concerned about anyone overhearing as I indulge in a little solo action.

It leaves me clean and ready for a long nap. But as I stretch out on the firm, white sofa where he slept, I'm hit with a fresh wave of his scent. Oh, blazes, that man is intoxicating.

I wish I knew what was holding him back. There's obviously some heavy chemistry between us. We're both single, and we're sharing this space for just a little while... it doesn't seem right not to explore and enjoy the moments while we have them.

I like him. A lot. But there's no future between us. Our worlds are too different. But sex can just be sex, and it makes no sense to resist something that could be amazing.

I suppose humans have a different view on all that. Virginity is some sacred thing, and with sexually transmitted diseases and unpredictable fertility cycles... yeah, I suppose I can see how casual sex might seem like a big decision.

Shifters don't have to worry about those issues. We're

immune to human diseases and don't seem to have any of our own. We also have very predictable fertility cycles, so getting pregnant by accident isn't even a remote possibility.

Virginity isn't some big thing to be cherished and celebrated. How can you get to know someone as a potential mate if you don't explore the physical aspects of the connection?

I was the only one of my friends who ever held back. I realize now that my mother's voice was always in my head, disguised as my conscience, and telling me that sex might make me accidentally choose the wrong mate.

Blazes, I was naïve to buy that.

I told Gideon I'm not a virgin. Technically, I've had sex twice, but I was so awkward and uncertain it barely counts. There were a few hot and heavy make-out sessions, but even then I always felt like I was risking something. Like being involved with someone casually might blind me to my true mate once he arrived. It had to be love at first sight, or nothing.

So naïve.

I sit up, shaking my head and scrubbing my hands over my face to clear my mind. I'm not here to lust after a human, or any male. I'm here to figure myself out so I can go back to the Meadow, or... I can't even think about the alternative.

And the clinic. Brom. I spoke to him the morning I left for my last patrol, then never showed up again. I can only imagine what he's thinking about my actions. I need to sort this out. I need to get back to the Meadow.

I close my eyes and give in to the Darkness. It coils around me like it was waiting for my return, and the sense that I'm not alone in this place is stronger than ever. My heart pounds in my chest, but I can't leave. I have to face this. I have to figure this out once and for all.

A knock at the door has me jolting back to reality as I jump to my feet. Gideon's back so soon? It's only been a few hours...

The door clicks and slides open, and a young woman gasps when she sees me standing in the middle of the room.

"Fuck!" She clasps a hand over her mouth as soon as the exclamation is out. "I'm so sorry! Oh, my goodness."

"Who are you?" I ask as that thread of jealousy coils in my belly yet again. She's a little younger than me, with long, inky hair and blue eyes as wide and bright as a summer sky.

"I'm so sorry... I'm Skye. I'm with housekeeping."

"A fitting name," I say, ignoring the surge of relief at the knowledge that she isn't here for Gideon. She tilts her head as if she doesn't understand my comment. "Your eyes... I was just thinking how they look as blue as a summer sky."

"Oh." She lifts a hand to her cheek as it turns a faint shade of pink, then shakes her head. "I can come back later. I didn't mean to interrupt. Mr. Grant rarely has guests, and he's in the system as out for the day. I'm so sorry to barge in like that."

"Mr. Grant?"

She looks at me like she doesn't understand my confusion, then her eyes crinkle as she suppresses a smile. "Elite Gideon Grant."

"Oh." Now it's my turn to blush. "I didn't know his last name."

She nods, not trying to hide her smile anymore. "It's okay, miss. We've all been there."

She winks, then turns to leave.

"Wait!"

She stops and looks at me with raised eyebrows.

"Come in. Don't let me stop you."

"Are you sure? It's no trouble to come back later..."

"I really don't mind." I already like this girl, and getting to know her a little more sounds like a great idea. I'm also not too eager to face the Darkness again.

She pauses for a second, then shrugs her shoulders and

pushes the door wide to pull in a cart filled with buckets and cleaning supplies.

"Do you clean his flat?" I hadn't given it any thought. Everything's so neat and clean. I just assumed Gideon was a very tidy person.

"I do." She answers with a casual tone while picking through her cart for specific items. "Most of the condos up here are full service."

"I guess I hadn't thought about it."

She looks at me with the same incredulous expression she gave me when I didn't know Gideon's name. "You're not from around here, I take it?"

"No."

"All people see when they look up here is wealth, privilege and power. But even the fine residents of Solar One shit and sweat like the rest of us. Someone's got to clean the toilets and do the laundry, and Lord knows they're all too busy to do it themselves."

I laugh as I wonder what she would say if I told her where I'm from. "I like you, Skye. I'm glad you came by."

Now it's her turn to laugh, and she shakes her head as she heads to the kitchen. It looks perfectly clean to me, but she starts at one end of the counter and spray's everything down with something that smells like plastic lemons.

"The last time I heard anything about Mr. Grant having company was when his niece stayed with him. Are you related?"

"No. I'm his... I'm a friend." I'm supposed to be his girlfriend, but it doesn't feel right to lie to her outright.

"I see." I can tell by the curve of her cheek that she's smiling. "Not that I'm suggesting the staff gossips or anything... but rumor has it Mr. Grant doesn't spend any time with female friends. Or male friends, for that matter. He hasn't been spotted with a date since he moved here a few years ago."

Not that I'd enjoy picturing him with another woman, but her claim doesn't bring me any satisfaction. I'm sure he just doesn't bring them here. Gideon's a warm, passionate person. He deserves some affection, some connection, some *happy for now*.

"I'm sure he dates... he's..." I let my voice trail off.

"Oh, I know. I've got eyes." She winks as she finishes her work in the kitchen.

I follow her to the bathroom. I'd like to offer to help, but she's so quick and efficient. I'd only be in the way. Watching her work makes me long for the clinic. Quiet days spent tidying and organizing. Busy days that turn into long evenings cleaning and taking inventory. I miss it all.

"I heard he was married before he moved here."

That sentence hits me like a rock. Married? "Oh, I-"

"No, don't." She cuts me off with a raised hand. "It's not my place to snoop. I'm just repeating rumors, but I don't want to invade his privacy. I shouldn't even be talking this much."

"No, it's okay. Gideon and I aren't... it's not serious. I'll be going home soon."

"Oh. Well, enjoy him while it lasts. And if you want to throw any juicy details my way..." Her eyebrows and hips do a little wiggle that gets her message across just fine.

I'd love to get to know Skye over some girl-talk. But I won't be here long enough to figure out if I can trust her enough to risk her guessing what I am.

"What about you? Do you have a ma-, a partner?"

I hold my breath for a second, but she doesn't seem to notice that I almost asked if she has a mate.

"Not really," she says. Her sly grin gives me the impression there's a good story behind that vague answer.

DARK CORNERS

"*J*appreciate your concern, but I assure you she's perfectly fine." Hope's mother adjusts her posture slightly in her chair, her hands folded together in her lap.

"She's never disappeared like this and-"

"Perhaps not in the short time you've known her, but my daughter can be a bit of a free spirit when the mood strikes her."

Damon nods, and I hope he senses that he's pushed the subject as far as Molly will tolerate with any amount of patience.

"It was good to meet you, Whisper." She turns her attention to me, and I smile.

"You too, Ms. Edwards."

"Call me Molly."

We came to her tent under the guise of *formally introducing* myself to Hope's parents, though I couldn't care less about formalities. I respect their position, such as it is, but I don't have any desire to align myself as one of her followers.

The real reason we're here is to gauge her reaction to our concerns about Hope. She doesn't know that we're aware Hope's in Moridian, taking some much-needed space while she sorts out her feelings about all this arranged-mating bullshit.

Damon had suspicions about things not being quite as they seemed, and I'm far better at reading people than he is. It's a skill I honed very intentionally. If you can read micro-expressions, you can learn far more about a person's intentions than they're choosing to say with words.

Molly might try to act as if Hope's absence is no big deal, but I don't think that's how she feels. I don't think she has a clue where her daughter is.

What I find a little unexpected is that she doesn't appear to be angry about it. Maybe she's just that good at playing her public persona.

"It seems, *Ms. Edwards*, that you're the only one who isn't concerned about Hope."

There's a flare of anger in her eyes. Maybe just an involuntary reaction to being not so subtly challenged. But instead of narrowing her gaze, or aligning her posture more directly with mine, she glances at her husband. It's quick, almost imperceptible, but I'm certain I see a flash of fear in her dark gaze.

Carl Edwards is suddenly far more interesting than he appeared a moment ago. Quietly whittling away at a shapeless chunk of wood, his docile, detached personality is no longer so convincing. The more I look at him, the more I see what I hadn't noticed before.

"You risked a lot to save Molly and create this place."

His eyes snap to mine, as his fingers continue to work away at the sliver of wood that seems to be transforming into nothing more than a smaller stick.

"No risk would have been too great to keep her safe." His pasted-on smile doesn't hide the caution in his eyes.

Not wanting to push my luck, I thank them both for their time and hospitality.

Out on the packed dirt between the tents, I thread my fingers in Damon's as we walk. He doesn't speak for a while, knowing me well enough to understand that I need a moment to review and sort my thoughts.

"What are you thinking?"

"I loved you from the moment I first saw you."

He stops, pulls me into his arms and presses his lips against mine. I lean into his warmth. I swear no matter how long I live, I'll never stop melting at this man's touch.

The people that witness our frequent displays of affection don't even bother me anymore. I didn't think I would be able to shake that instinct to hide, but it turns out it didn't take long at all.

This place is another world. A better world. And it deserves to be protected at all costs.

"It wasn't a romantic love, at first. We were partners for years and I loved you. When you took human form, I resisted accepting that the man in front of me was who you really were. It took me far too long to realize the full scope of how wrong we treat Shifters."

"You were told the lie all your life."

"Exactly." We reach our tent, but even once we're sitting side by side on Damon's cot, I still keep my voice low. "Carl wasn't a Protector, so he didn't personally know any Shifters. He worked in the lab, supposedly as a custodian who also processed *biological waste*. Yet, six months after rescuing Molly, he takes one look at her human face and changes his entire outlook on life? He rescues more, and they run off to start a new community, where he takes up wood carving and lets Molly run the show."

He narrows his eyes, considering the angle I'm presenting. At face value, it's a mildly suspicious story, but believable if you factor in the power of love at first sight.

But we've lived it. Love isn't enough to immediately over-throw a lifetime of conditioning.

"No one here seems to question it."

"Why would they? How it began doesn't change the fact that it's working. People here feel safe and free to be them-selves. But either I was even more selfish and blind than I thought, or something's not right with Mr. Alpha's story."

Damon lays back on the bed, folding his arms behind his head. "Does it even matter? Are we just stirring up trouble?"

"He said no risk would have been too great to keep her safe, but he didn't even glance at his wife when he said it."

"What does that mean?"

"It means he probably wasn't talking about her. But Hope wasn't planned. They didn't get pregnant until after he was already in hiding."

"Sure, but they didn't go into Morwood until after Hope was born."

I flop down beside him, and his hand immediately moves to rest on my stomach. Am I just stirring up trouble? Am I so conditioned to finding abuse and corruption, that I'll manufac-ture it where it doesn't exist?

His fingers move against my skin, and I cover his hand with mine. We're together, with a lifetime of possibilities in front of us. And we're not the only people who have a future that wouldn't be possible without the Meadow.

I'm not being paranoid. I'm being a Protector. This place deserves protection, and that means poking around in dark corners to find the threats before they're strong enough to hurt us.

KOBA

"*I*t's time to end this. Quietly, if possible, before the public gets wind of the full scope."

"I'm not sure I follow..."

Elder Samuel didn't seem the least bit surprised that I returned without usable intel. In fact, he wasn't interested in my report beyond confirmation that I'd found no signs of a Shifter stronghold.

"The Shifter program needs to be reset. We have to act fast, before this gets out of our control." He pulls his wire-framed glasses off his face, pinching the bridge of his nose as he leans back into his chair. "We can't have the Centaurians thinking we're blaming them for this. The official story will be that BioSol botched something."

Reset? "What are my orders, Elder?"

He looks up at me from behind his desk, scrutinizing my expression for a moment. He'll find no emotion there.

"The Shifters need to be destroyed. All of them."

What the fuck?

"All of them?"

"Is there a problem?"

"No, Elder..." Yes. Yes, there's a fucking problem. "The logistics of putting down all the active Shifters. I don't see how we can do that without causing a public-"

"I'm not interested in hashing out the details now. There are six of you on the task force. You can meet on Monday and figure out the most effective way forward."

He swipes his comm a few times, and mine vibrates in my pocket. A list of five names. All of them Elite's I've worked with in the past, not that there are many I haven't worked with.

"Enjoy your weekend off. This job will keep you busy for a while, I suspect."

THE SOUND of the door opening jars me out of a heavy nap, and my heart does a strange, sputtering dance as Gideon steps through the door. His face is creased with some troubling emotion, but when he looks in my direction a smile lights his features.

"You're a sight for sore eyes."

I tip my head at the strange greeting, but then I clue in that I'm still in my wolf form. After a few more failed attempts at getting my bearings in the Darkness, I was too exhausted to keep trying. This form's much better at many things, including napping when my mind would rather be worrying.

Besides, after Skye reminded me that Tarek hangs around here in bear form, I'm not so concerned about my fur getting on the furniture.

Instead of shifting back to my human form, I push off the sofa and walk toward him. He crouches down to eye level, his hands reaching out to touch me. I lean into the delicious sensation of his fingers threading through the thick fur at my neck.

"Beautiful."

His smile fades into the emotion that was troubling him when he first entered the flat. He drops his hands and I shift to my human form.

He stands, and I follow his lead. Taking a deep breath to summon some confidence, I reach up to touch his neck as he did to my wolf. He jerks as my fingertips brush his skin, but then stays still. I touch the top of the trail of implant tattoos, following it down to where it ends at his collarbone.

I'd like to ask him what they all mean, but I'm not sure I really want to know. I've heard plenty of stories about Protectors and their artificial enhancements.

He takes my wrist, so gentle despite the strength he must possess, and pulls me away from his neck.

That troubled expression remains, and I realize I've been so caught up in the thrill of seeing him again, that I didn't even think about the importance of his task today. He went to see the Elders. To report back that he found nothing of Shifters in Morwood.

"Is everything okay?"

My chest tightens as his silence lingers on. Images of all the things that could have gone wrong playing through my mind as I hold my breath.

"Everything's fine," he says after a too long pause. The smile he offers doesn't reach his eyes.

"You spoke with the Elders?"

"Yeah." He walks past me, heading to the kitchen. "Briefly. I informed them I found nothing."

He pulls a glass out of the cupboard, filling it at the sink.

"And they believed you? They didn't question?"

He takes a long drink, sets the glass in the sink, and runs a hand through his hair.

"Everything's fine. Just a few loose ends on my mind.

Nothing for you to worry about." Another shallow smile. "I need a shower. I won't be long."

He doesn't make eye contact with me as he disappears into his bedroom, reappearing with an armful of clean clothes before closing himself in the bathroom.

I think he needed an excuse to avoid my questions more than he needed a shower.

An unpleasant weight settles in my gut. He's keeping something from me. Just like his niece's story, it's probably none of my business.

I wanted to ask about Skye's mention of him being married. Even if it's also none of my business, he should know that I know.

I hear the shower turn on, and a new feeling settles even lower in my belly. Does he really have to shower every day? That seems excessive.

Oh blazes, the mental image of him under that water is way too appealing. The same shower I thoroughly enjoyed while thinking of him. Why did I have to get all proper and look away back at the lake? It would have been well worth the awkward aftermath to have fewer blanks for my imagination to fill in.

I need some air.

I hum a little tune to drown out the sound of the running water as I head for the balcony. The cool air fills my lungs as soon as the doors slide open, but the Presence tingles under my skin. I'm not alone.

A huge, gray mass of feathers drops from above. My instinct to shift is immediate, but I resist. The massive bird lands just inches from me, tipping its head to regard me with piercing black eyes.

I slink backward, through the door and toward the bathroom. I'm useless in this form, but showing myself as a Shifter could cause worlds of trouble depending on who this Shifter's loyalties lie with.

I'm halfway there when the bird shudders, melting into the form of a huge, white bear. I hurry my retreat, and he starts toward me with long, heavy strides. His black eyes are unblinking, his nostrils flared.

The Presence moves painfully fast, up my spine and into my skull with a burst of pain. The bear shakes its mighty head, growling as it speeds up.

I reach the bathroom, groping for the door handle without turning around. It's not locked. I slip into the steamy warmth.

"Gideon!" I whisper-shout over the sound of the shower, as his scent immediately surrounds me. I keep my back to the shower, holding the door closed with both my hands as if that could keep a beast that size out. "There's a polar bear in your flat."

The water turns off, and a moment later Gideon's thick, and very wet, arm comes into my view as he presses his palm against the door.

"Move."

I do as he says, backing away from the door, and sweet blazes I don't even care about the bear anymore. Gideon is dripping wet. His hair is plastered against his head as water runs in thin rivulets over his body, soaking into the white towel tied around his waist.

He reaches up to the mirror above the sink, placing the pad of his thumb against a top corner. A light blinks behind the glass, and the corner of the mirror opens like a door. Reaching inside the hidden cupboard, he pulls out a gun.

I don't know a thing about weapons, but I'm sure even a bear Shifter will think twice about picking a fight with the person holding that.

A quick check of the weapon, while I drink in the view of

so much skin, and Gideon pulls the bathroom door open. I walk with him, keeping a few paces back, as he approaches the bear with the gun leveled at its head.

"Koba." Gideon addresses the bear with a wary but familiar tone. "What the fuck are you doing here, buddy? Where's Cade?"

The bear swings his big head to study Gideon, then returns his attention to me. The look in his eyes is unsettling, and I realize he's an unawakened Shifter. He doesn't know he's anything more than an accessory to his human master. My heart aches for him, even as the Presence flares, crawling up my spine in response to the possible threat.

The bear keeps staring, inhaling deep breaths that expand and contract his massive ribcage in a steady rhythm. He knows I'm something different, but does he realize how? Would he even have the ability to comprehend the possibility that I could be a female Shifter?

The weapon in Gideon's hands makes a clicking sound, and the bear walks toward me again.

"Stand down, Koba. Last warning. I'll follow you to Cade, but you've got to back off."

Koba's so focused on me, he doesn't even react to Gideon's warning. He keeps coming. I don't think he means any harm, but he's going to force Gideon to make good on his threat.

The Presence flares behind my eyes, and Koba recoils instantly. He makes a pitiful whining noise as he scrambles to back away, his enormous body plowing into the sofa and pushing it across the floor like it's weightless.

I feel something new.

The Presence isn't just claiming its foothold in my skull, it's gripping my chest with an emotion that isn't mine. I don't know how, but I can feel Koba. It's not fear he's responding to as he backs away toward the balcony, keeping his eyes averted. It's something else...

Alpha. The word comes to me, not like hearing his thoughts, but more like a feeling.

He backs onto the balcony and shifts to his winged form to take off into the sky.

My knees are weak as I grip the back of the sofa for support. The Presence receded the moment Koba left, but my entire body is still humming in the aftermath of that crazy connection. I've always kind of absorbed the emotions of others, but this was far more acute. I *felt* his thoughts.

Gideon steps through the door, his gun held steady until he's sure the threat's gone. He leans down, retrieving something from the floor. A piece of paper. A message.

"What does it say?"

Gideon folds the paper, locking the door before walking silently back to the bathroom. He returns the weapon to its secret compartment behind the mirror, leaving the note with it.

He closes the bathroom door just enough to block my view of him. I hear the rustle of clothing and the sound of a zipper before the door opens again, and he faces me with a stern expression and thick arms folded across his bare chest. Anger surges, even as my traitorous eyes drop to his naked stomach and the v-cut of his hips that disappears beyond the waist of his pants.

"What does it say?"

"What the fuck just happened?"

"Nothing, I..." The words die in my throat. I don't want to lie to him. He deserves better than that, but how can I explain what I don't even understand? I fumble for an excuse or a diversion, but all I have is the truth. "I'm not... just me. I... I hurt people."

Tears slip down my cheeks. It's barely a confession, but it's the first time I've spoken anything about this out loud. The first time I've wanted to. I close my eyes. I can't bear to see the disgust on his face.

I jump when his hand touches my cheek. I keep my eyes squeezed shut as his thumb brushes my skin, over my cheek, then across my mouth. My lips part on a sigh, because even with the weight of this moment, his touch is like moonlight on the lake. A peaceful escape. A beautiful distraction.

Then he kisses me. It's not tentative. It's not impulsive. It's intentional, and real, and deep, and his arms are around me as my hands glide over his biceps, his shoulders. His body is steel and silk and I want to touch all of him.

He breaks the kiss, but I feel the loss for only a moment before his lips are on my neck. His mouth burns a trail down to my collarbone, and I raise my hands above my head as he grasps the hem of my shirt, pulling it up... and then back down.

I open my eyes, and his expression takes my breath away. I don't know what happened to this beautiful man, but the pain that's laced through the lust makes my heart break.

HAPPY FOR NOW

I'm losing control.

Hope walks across the room, smelling like all my dirty dreams after a long bath. An unnecessary bath, since all she has to do is shift to be clean. She says it's relaxing. She's completely oblivious to how much the thought of her in there drives me crazy. Just like yesterday, she's heading out onto the balcony to dry her hair in the morning breeze.

When she closes the door, I adjust my cock to a more comfortable angle and down the rest of my coffee. Time to head to the gym and put this energy to good use. I could have gone during her three-hour soak, but the more excuses we have to be in separate rooms, the better.

It's been two days since Koba dropped in on us. Two days since I kissed her for the fourth time and almost…

I can't go there. I can't let her get closer to me, knowing how appalled she'll be when she learns what I'm keeping from her.

But she's keeping secrets, too. Whatever she did to Koba, she did something similar to Luke back at the lake. I don't know what she's hiding, but I suspect it's the real reason she's committed herself to this metal cage.

But it's not her that's making me lose control.

I've been hiding what I know about Shifters since Damon first showed me; covering for Tarek, for both our sakes, and now hiding a Shifter female in my flat.

Now, I'm on the task force to kill them all, and I can't refuse because it would show my hand and some other asshole would get the job. I need to be part of it if I have any chance of stopping it. But if I try to stop it, it'll only show my hand... and round and round I go.

Completely fucking out of control.

The one thing I can do is keep her safe. That's why, after I get back from the gym, I'm taking Hope's ass home. I don't care how much she protests. It doesn't matter how curious I am to know what her deal is.

She's leaving. Today.

～

IT'S NO USE. I've tried everything. The Darkness doesn't even scare me anymore, as I sink into it for the thousandth time this weekend. I can't get any deeper. There's no epiphany. No evil spirits.

Was it all in my head?

No. What I did to Luke, to Mother, to Koba... that wasn't just in my head.

I need to understand it, and I need to tell Gideon. I came so close after Koba left. I wanted to explain everything, but I just couldn't find the words. I still can't find the words, which is why I've resorted to avoiding him all weekend. Not a simple task in his small flat.

I suspect he's attempting the same, because after my ridiculously long bath, he takes off for the afternoon at the gym. Same as yesterday. I'm sure he'd go to work if he could, but it just happens to be his weekend off.

We've barely spoken. We haven't touched.

And I haven't been able to learn anything new about my problem.

It's time for me to go. Not home, I'm not ready for that yet. But away from here. Away from him. Maybe, when I'm not so distracted by my libido, the Presence will be more active and the Darkness will reveal more secrets.

But first, I need to explain myself to him. The whole truth. Not just about my issues, but also my feelings for him. I don't want to leave without exploring this crazy, unexpected attraction. I know he feels it too. If we stop denying it, we can enjoy it and move on.

My heart threatens to beat through my chest when I hear his key in the door. I smooth my hair, taking deep breaths and summoning as much courage as I can manage.

"I need to leave."

He pauses in the doorway as his eyes search my face. His hair's damp from showering at the gym, and the veins in his arms are popping from the exercise.

He hangs up his key, drops his gym bag, and crosses the floor until he's within arm's reach.

"Yes. You do. I think that's for the best."

I nod, ignoring the pinch in my chest.

"But I don't want to leave without exploring this. Us." He braces, his jaw clenching. I hurry my words. "I don't want any promises. I don't need any explanations. We're two adults who are clearly…"

He drowns my words in a bruising kiss, his hands gripping my head as he devours my mouth like a starving man. I'm helpless for only a moment, then I'm right there with him.

My hands slide under his shirt, equally hungry and desperate for more contact, but he breaks the kiss. Pressing his forehead against mine, he breathes in heavy pants that make his chest stretch the fabric of his shirt.

"Hope," my name sounds like an apology. "You don't know me. You can't want this."

I step back, waiting for him to meet my eyes. "Do you want me?"

"Fuck, yes."

I pull my shirt over my head. I don't give him time to object. My jeans follow in a heap on the floor. My bra. My panties. My socks. I stand before him naked, as his pale eyes rake over me, bright with lust. But his body is rigid. Every muscle is tense, and guarded, even as his obvious arousal strains against his jeans.

I want him so badly it hurts. But more than his body, I want to understand what broke him. What made him so scared of his own pleasure... because that's what this is. Even back at the lake, when he touched my face and recoiled with disgust... it was his own desire that disgusted him.

"Come to bed with me."

His eyes snap to mine, his jaw clenched so tight it has to be painful.

"I won't take anything you aren't ready to give. I just want your hands on my skin. Your heat against my back."

Something cracks in his expression, the tension melting as the heat burns brighter. He steps toward me, and when his hands grip my hips, I bite my lip to keep from whimpering with need.

I'll respect his boundaries, whatever they may be, but it'll be the hardest thing I've ever done.

He lowers his face to mine, a soft kiss brushing my lips that only fuels the fire raging inside me.

I shudder as his lips press against my shoulder. Then the opposite shoulder. My collarbone. His breath is hot against my skin as his hands move from my hips, up my sides until they cup my breasts. His thumbs brush across the hardened peaks, and a needy moan is torn from my chest.

I hold my breath, afraid the sound of my arousal might scare him away.

"There's so much you don't know about me, Hope. Things that would make you want nothing to do with me. Things that will make you regret this."

"Can't we just be happy for now?"

He kisses me softly, then drops to his knees. He presses a kiss to my navel, then one hip, and the other. Then his kiss is pressed to the apex of my thighs, and I'm completely shameless as I scoot my feet apart, opening myself to whatever he wants to do. Wherever he wants to take this.

The firm heat of his tongue slides over my clit, and I cry out as I grab fistfuls of his hair to anchor myself. His hands grip my backside, holding me steady as his tongue delves deep, then returns to flick over my clit before delving again.

"You taste fucking delicious." His voice is a growl against my sex, and I shudder with the intensity of it.

His tongue claims me again, finding a pressure and rhythm that winds me up so fast I don't have the chance to warn him before my orgasm tears through me. I rip apart at the seams, flying in all directions at once. Falling, and soaring, and oblivious to anything but this impossible pleasure.

When the pieces of me come together again, I'm floating. I'm in Gideon's arms as he carries me cradled against him.

He lays me on the bed, and I've never felt so satisfied. And so hungry for more. I reach for him, and there's no hesitation as he pulls his shirt over his head, then crawls over me to kiss me breathless. His hunger is obvious, desperate, and I want to give him what he needs. I press my palms against the hard planes of his chest, moving down over the contours of his stomach. My fingers reach the waist of his jeans, but he pulls away from my reach, moving his kiss over my jaw, down my neck, kissing a burning trail until his mouth covers a sensitive nipple. I moan and arch my back like a wanton thing as he nips and sucks first one breast, then the other.

I want him inside me so desperately, I bite my lip to keep from begging. Even in this state of delirious arousal, I know he's giving me a precious part of him. I know if I push him, he could retreat.

But he knows what I want. He knows what my body craves, and as his mouth works sinful magic on my chest, his hand slides over my stomach to apply pressure exactly where I need it. Fingers slide inside my core, curling to find that elusive place, and I'm torn into oblivion again as an orgasm hits me so hard, I'm screaming his name.

~

THIS WOMAN.

I run my fingers through the fine, moonlit waves of her hair. I brush the full curve of her lips, reddened from my kisses. I trail my hand down her body, memorizing every line and curve. Every inch of perfect skin.

She gave herself to me, without reservation or expectation. Happy for now.

I push off the bed. She whimpers when my body heat leaves her side, but I tuck her into the blankets and she settles again. I stand over her for a moment, watching her face relaxed in sleep. A hint of a smile plays at the corner of her lips.

An image flashes behind my eyes, of me, naked and spent, wrapped around her body as we bask in the shared afterglow. I've never wanted that with anyone as much as I want it with her.

I'm aware I have a problem. My avoidance of sex is unhealthy. Psychological scar tissue. But when Hope offered herself, when she pulled off her clothes and offered everything while making it clear she expected nothing, I thought for a moment I could... that maybe now, with this woman, it could be okay to move on.

What the fuck was I thinking? Lily sure as hell can't move on. Why should I? Maybe I should start seeing Dr. Blake again... fuck. What am I even thinking? I understand the psychology. I don't want to *heal*. She's dead. I killed her. Why the fuck would I deserve to get better or to move on with my life?

Hope doesn't know me. She doesn't deserve the regret that's inevitable when she learns the full story.

I turn away, heading for the bathroom, but her hand on my wrist stops me.

"Gideon?"

"I'm sorry. I didn't mean to wake you."

"I didn't mean to fall asleep. Are you okay?"

I hate the concern that darkens her violet eyes. I crouch beside the bed and kiss her. Soft and slow.

"Do you need help getting back to sleep?" My voice is a whisper against her lips, and she shudders at the suggestion.

"Will you keep me warm?" She pulls back to look me in the eyes, and all I want to do is give her everything she wants.

"I can do that." I crawl back onto the bed, settling in beside her with my hips at an angle so she can't feel how painfully hard she's made me.

I pull her into my arms, against my chest, rubbing her back

as I force my mind to focus on work. It's damn impossible with the way her fingers are playing across my stomach, tracing invisible shapes and patterns.

"Can I touch you?"

I swear my cock's going to punch a hole through my jeans. I should tell her no. I should tell her everything, so she'll stop asking me. Stop wanting me.

But I can't.

It's more than my personal issues now. Tomorrow's my meeting with the core team; the lucky six who get to murder an entire population of Shifters.

And then there's Cade's note. His summons to a meeting before the official one, his chosen mode of communication making it clear he doesn't want the Elders involved.

Hope's lips graze my chest, pulling me from my thoughts. The sensation goes straight to my cock as she covers my skin with soft kisses punctuated by the wet heat of her tongue. She makes a small noise, halfway between a purr and a growl, and I'm helpless to resist her.

I shift onto my back, and she covers my stomach with more unhurried kisses, while her fingers roam over my arms and ribs.

She makes little noises as she explores; soft sounds of pleasure as she seems to enjoy the feel and taste of me as much as I enjoyed her.

And fuck, did I enjoy tasting her.

There's a gentle tug at my waist, and I look down to see her watching me, a playful glint in her eyes as her teeth pull on a piece of denim at the button of my jeans.

She's asking in the sexiest, sweetest way possible. There isn't a single part of me that wants to stop her now.

I pop the button and lower the zipper, lifting my hips for her to pull my jeans down. When my cock springs free, her gasp gives way to an inhuman growl.

For the first time in a very long while, I'm grateful to have been blessed with more than my fair share of inches and girth.

Her hands are on me, soft and tentative. Then her mouth. Her tongue. She's exploring my cock like she did the rest of me, and I'm lost in fucking bliss like I've never felt before.

I've gotten my share of blow jobs, when a quickie in the back of a bar or my truck was my definition of a successful night. But it's been a long while, and this is something else entirely. This is a new level of oral perfection.

I'm torn between closing my eyes to bask in the sensations and watching her face as she works her magic on my body. Her perfect mouth stretched around my cock is the most erotic thing I've ever seen. I don't think... I can't...

"I'm coming." I expect her to jump back at my growled warning, but she digs her nails into my hips and takes me so deep there's no doubt what she wants.

I let go. Gripping the headboard and letting her hear how she's made me feel, I come harder than I knew possible. And it doesn't stop. She keeps working my body as the best orgasm of my life just won't quit.

When she kisses her way back up my body, my mind's blown and my body's spent. She cuddles in close, and I want to say something, but there's nothing that would do justice to the way she's made me feel.

I hold her tighter, kick my pants off the rest of the way, and adjust us until as much of me is touching as much of her as possible.

CONFESSIONS

aking up like this, with this man in this place, I feel like a new woman. Wrapped in his arms, surrounded by his strength... We didn't make love, but the pleasure we shared and the night spent tangled together in sleep was the most incredible thing I've ever experienced.

A sleepy rumble vibrates his chest as he stirs, and I'm taken back to last night. The taste of him. The obvious pleasure he felt at my touch. Even if he never wants to have actual sex, I'd be content if I could be with him like that every night. Make him come like that; his entire body flexing as the headboard cracks in his fists and he roars with the intensity of it.

I clench my thighs around his leg to ease the pressure that's building at the mere thought of it; of him, and of all the possibilities for nights ahead.

But it's foolish daydreams. There's no future for us. He saw what I did to Koba, and I meant what I said. I'm going to tell him everything. Maybe, just maybe, he'll feel comfortable telling me about the thing that haunts him.

"Good morning," he says, his voice thick from sleep as his hand moves against my back.

"Good morning." I run my fingers along his skin, from his chest, down under the cover and over his hip, then back again.

It's comfortable. Ordinary. For a moment I imagine that he'll kiss me and roll me onto my back to enjoy a little morning pleasure.

He presses a kiss to the top of my head, but then pushes to the edge of the bed and stands. I'm helpless to do anything but stare as he moves across the room, naked and every bit as beautiful as I pictured he would be. I watch him openly as he dresses, captivated by every smooth flex of muscle under silky skin.

When he pulls a clean shirt over his head, I slide out of the bed. He watches me as I gather my clothes from where they fell last night. I return to the bedroom to dress, and I make sure to move slow and deliberate so he can look his fill.

When I'm combing my hair back into a pony, our eyes meet for the first time this morning. The smile he gives me makes my heart soar, and he welcomes me into his arms for a slow, deep kiss.

"Coffee?"

I nod eagerly, more enthused by the promise of time with him then I am about the drink.

He disappears into the bathroom, and I shift in and out of my wolf form to clean my clothes and body. When he emerges a few minutes later, I take my turn. The aroma of coffee and toast greets me when I'm done, along with his smile.

"Will you tell me what happened with Koba?"

We sit at the table, a warm mug cradled in my hands. His question isn't unexpected, but I was hoping we could enjoy a little more *normal* before we got to it.

A deep breath steadies my shaking nerves.

"There's a Presence inside me. I'm not sure if it's part of me, or something else." I try to gauge his reaction, but his face gives nothing away. "I think I can connect with other minds. I can feel their emotions, and I can hurt them sometimes. When I'm emotional, I feel it crawling like a living thing. If I'm angry, or threatened, it takes hold of me and it hurts people, like you saw with Koba. It's getting stronger and I... I can't always control it."

He takes a slow sip of his coffee, his expression thoughtful but not disgusted or disbelieving. His reaction, or lack of one, gives me confidence.

"Have you ever talked to anyone about it?"

"No. But I think my parents saw something. I argued with Mother, and the Presence flared. It's part of why I had to leave. I don't know what they'll do if they realize how defective I am. I'm supposed to be their pride and joy, the first natural Shifter... but I'm something else. I might be dangerous."

"You're not dangerous." He says it with such confidence I almost believe him.

"Did you feel it? When Koba was here?"

"No. Nothing."

"I'm not imagining it. I know it sounds like magic or my imagination..."

"It sounds like BioSol."

"That's not possible. I've never even been there. I wasn't born in the lab."

"Can you use it on me?"

"I can't do it on command. I have to be feeling something real. It's never seemed to work against humans, anyway."

He tips his head back and forth as if weighing options. "Well, maybe something they tinkered with in your mother. Who knows."

I lower my eyes and set my coffee down. That's just it. Who knows? Will I ever figure out what's wrong with me? I don't even know where to start. He reaches out and takes my hand in his, and I cling to him like an anchor.

But I'm not done being honest. My next words might be the end of this moment, but I have to come clean about what I know.

"I heard you were married."

He sucks in a sharp breath, his hand turning to stone. I thread my fingers through his, soaking up the feel of his skin against mine.

"Skye told me she thought you'd been married before you moved here. A few years ago. And you haven't dated since."

He lets out a humorless chuckle. "The chatty one. I should've warned you about her."

I smile at his description. "I liked her. She was fun to talk to. And she didn't want to gossip, she just mentioned it. I think she assumed I knew."

The last thing I want is to get Skye in trouble, or cause Gideon to think poorly of her.

"It's fine. I was married." He pauses, and I let that simple fact sink in. He told me he'd never been in love. That he didn't even believe in the concept. But he was married? "Lily was... well... I barely knew her. We got married because she was pregnant."

My lungs constrict as his revelation takes the air out of the room. I try not to show how much it affects me.

A child? "Where are they?"

"She died. With the baby."

The room spins as tears sting the backs of my eyes. I open my mouth to offer a response, but I can't come up with any words that seem even remotely enough.

"It was my fault." His words carry the weight of confession. Of years of guilt and shame.

"What happened?" His eyes hold pure, raw pain. It cuts me

to see him this way, but I want to understand. And I think maybe he needs to talk about it.

"We were barely even dating. It was a casual, Friday night regular kind of thing. We didn't even know each other beyond the bar and my backseat."

I swallow the lump in my throat. The image of him with someone, having sex so casually and openly... I know he was a different person. I can't compare the man with me now, to the man he was.

"We got really fucked up one night and decided we should get married. Even went online and filled out the paperwork. Felt like the best idea I'd ever had.

I told her since we were going to be husband and wife soon, we didn't need to bother using a condom. She said I was crazy. Said there was no way she was risking getting pregnant. But she was on the pill anyway, so I pushed. I pressured her until she gave in."

I can't picture him like that. Behaving that way. "Sounds like you were young, and irresponsible, but-"

"When she found out she was pregnant, she came to tell me she was getting an abortion. I don't know why she even told me... by then, we'd forgotten about the whole marriage thing and gone back to our usual Friday nights. I assumed she wanted my help, but what she wanted was for me to tell her I agreed; to make her conscious a little clearer before she went through with it.

I pressured her again. It wasn't my body, she wasn't even my girlfriend, but I pressured her to keep the baby. We still had the paperwork on file, so I dropped down on one knee and asked her to marry me sober. That week, we found a little place on the edge of the Solar and I paid double to get us moved in fast. Two weeks later, we were married."

He shifts in his seat, his hand still on mine even though his gaze is focused inward. I keep quiet, barely breathing for fear of interrupting.

"She was happy for a couple months, until the pregnancy really started to show. Then she got angry. She didn't want a family. Never had. We didn't have a thing in common, and she kept telling me that all I cared about was the baby, not her."

"I'm sure that wasn't true..." He flinches, and I regret speaking up.

"No. She was right. We argued all the time. She refused to eat. She kept drinking. I tried everything to get her to take care of herself... but not because I loved her. Because I needed her. She said she was nothing but an incubator to me, and I didn't see the truth in her words until they were both gone."

He stops, and the silence between us is painfully loud. I can't reconcile the man in his story with the one I've come to know. I have so many questions, but I can tell he's done for now.

"You're not that person anymore, Gideon. I know you, and you're-"

"That is who I am, Hope. I use people to get what I want. I used Lily, abandoned her emotionally, and they died because of it. My son died because I was too selfish to love his mother. I can't put myself in that position again. I can't risk making that mistake again."

I can't hold back the tears any longer, and when they spill down my cheeks, he pushes himself up and away from the table. I want to comfort him, I want to convince him he's changed, learned from his mistakes, and that we can do better.

"I have to go out."

He can't leave. If we don't finish this now, he might never open up to me again. I have to know the rest, so I can help him...

"Koba's message was to meet Cade at eight sharp. He

doesn't want the Elder's knowing, otherwise he would have texted me. Does Koba know you're a Shifter?"

I wipe the tears from my face. I don't know how he can just say all that, then brush it off and move on like nothing. But that's not fair. He's been living with all this for so long. Lily and their baby. His sister and niece, too. He's been putting his pain aside to do his job for years.

"I don't know. I don't think so... but he recognized something. He... his thoughts were... it didn't make any sense."

"Stay here. I'll be back as soon as I can." He heads for the door.

"I'm coming with you."

SHAKE IT OFF

"What the fuck are they doing here, Gideon?"

"I didn't set it up. How many are here?"

"Five so far." Kelsey hisses as she clicks her fingernails on the bar.

So, Cade's summons wasn't for a private meeting. This smells more and more like an ambush.

"I'll deal with it."

"You better. Five fucking Elites in my bar. How can this be a safe place for Shifters, if their Elites are hanging around?"

"Keep an eye on her for me?"

Kelsey's expression softens as she looks over my shoulder. Hope's sitting at a booth, since making her stay in the truck was just as impossible as making her stay at my apartment.

"You shouldn't have brought her anywhere near those men."

"She's not very good at taking no for an answer." Bringing her anywhere near this little meeting feels all kinds of wrong, but aside from hitting her with a tranq, there was no convincing her to see reason.

Kelsey raises an eyebrow as a smile plays at the corners of her mouth. "I bet she isn't."

I give her a look that says *shut the fuck up*, and she laughs.

"I'll keep an eye on her, but I'm short staffed for breakfast today."

I thank her as I look back at Hope. She's watching me, her face etched with concern. My memory returns to last night. To the warmth of her body in my arms, the way she tasted, the way she sounded. Her cheeks redden, and I know her thoughts are right with mine.

I give her a smile, hoping it will ease her worry, and she returns one that makes my heart melt a little more.

In the back room, five pairs of eyes greet me when I enter. Cade stands against the wall, arms crossed, dressed in his tactical. Darius and Lock sit on opposite arms of a sofa. Connor's on a chair, leaning with his elbows on his knees. Jude's on the floor, his back against the pool table as he tosses the eight-ball from hand to hand.

We're all dressed for combat today.

"Boys."

I've worked with each of these men at one time or another. The six of us make up the team that's supposed to be meeting this afternoon.

"Elite Gideon." Cade greets me with a guarded expression, giving me no hint of what Koba told him about Hope.

The silence in the room is loaded, and I get the impression it's no accident that I'm the last one here.

"What the fuck is this?" I aim the question at Cade.

"We're taking a vote." His mouth curls up on one side as he uncrosses his arms. "To see which one of us gets to put the bullet between Tarek's eyes."

This is a test. They have an opinion about the Elder's decision, and they want to see where I stand.

"Probably should be Darius. Then we'd be even for what I did to Maverick when I tracked him into Morwood."

Darius is on his feet and in my face in an instant. Tapping into his Stim implant out of pure emotion; not the reaction of someone who views Shifters as expendable assets.

"Back the fuck off, man." I give him a shove that's weak enough to let him know I'm not looking for a fight. "I'm just testing the water, same as you."

Darius backs off, but they're all on their feet now. Even Jude, who grips the eight-ball like it was seconds from being embedded in my skull. His definition of a fair fight has always been a little flexible.

"Why are we here, boys? Lay it out for me. Nothing you say goes beyond these walls, and I expect the same in return."

Cade nods, but it's Connor who speaks up first. "I'm not putting Fury down."

"Axel's off limits, too." Lock crosses his arms.

"Our orders are to kill all Shifters," I remind them.

"Fuck our orders." Jude. Always on the verge of going off the rails. "The Elder's can go-"

"Shut up, man." Cade cuts him off. "No one here is suggesting we go against the Elders. But I think we can all agree that this job won't be easy, or quick. So we agree right now, all of us, that our Shifters go last. That's the deal."

"And you think they'll just wait in line, watching you kill their brothers?"

"Brothers? They don't give a fuck about each other one way or another."

So that confirms Koba's not awakened. And he clearly doesn't know about Shifters taking human form and breaking their bonds to become independent. So why the fuck are we here at Kelsey's?

"We take out BioSol Labs." Cade throws the idea out, and everyone falls silent.

"The Elder's will never sign off on that," I assure him. "Too much tech comes out of there. It'll piss off too many players."

"Not the whole lab. Just the Shifter program. We go in nice and polite, during office hours, and give the orders to the techs to start euthanizing the specimens."

"It's in line with what the Elder's want," I agree. "And it gives us a chance to question the scientists, get their take on the cleanest way to do this."

"Maybe we can find a better solution, or at least an explanation, before we resort to turning our weapons on the poor bastards." Connor never had a stomach for violence. Why he ended up in this line of work is beyond me.

"We're not looking for a better solution." I cross my arms, looking at each of them in turn. "The Elder's want the Shifter program reset. So that's what we do. We clear out the lab, then we work our way through the Protectors as fast and quiet as possible. Most won't have a stomach for it, but we'll work in pairs. One to put the Shifter down, one to deal with its bond-mate. We'll put him out for a little nap if it comes to that."

"Fuck, dude. That's harsh." Jude sets the eight-ball down, resting his hands on his hips and looking a little green around the gills.

"What did you expect to come of this?" I lock my eyes on Cade's. "Did you seriously think a secret meeting would end with us changing the Elder's minds, or planning a coup?"

"I don't know, man. You tell me."

"What the fuck is that supposed to mean?"

Cade keeps eye contact, and it's clear he knows something. He organized this meeting. He planned it here for a reason. But he doesn't elaborate, and I'm not sure if the others know whatever it is he thinks he knows.

"Go the fuck home." I say to them all. "We'll work out the rest of the details this afternoon, at HQ. No more of this underground shit. Got it?"

They all acknowledge, and one by one they file out. Cade's last, and he steps up close.

"I didn't peg you for such a cold bastard."

"I have my orders. Same as you."

"We wouldn't be the first military in history to commit genocide in the name of the greater good."

Fuck. This guy's on my last nerve. I can't tell if he's being genuine, or if he's baiting me. The fact that I can't tell says plenty enough.

"You can take that up with the Elders, Elite. Be my guest. But I don't want to hear that shit again. I'm no fucking vegan, and neither are you. I might not enjoy butchering cows, but I sure as fuck like a good steak."

He nods, but I don't miss the twitch at the corner of his mouth.

When I'm alone, I sink down onto a chair. I need a minute before I go out there and face Hope. I can't tell her any of this. She'd never understand. Fuck, if there was another way...

There isn't. This won't stop. No matter what side of the line I stand on, lives will be lost.

The biggest threat to the Meadow right now is Shifters waking up and heading into the forest. If there's no more Shifters to awaken, then there's no one to lead the Elders to the Meadow. They can stay hidden. It might not keep them safe forever, but it will buy them a lot more time.

There's no part of me that enjoys the prospect of taking innocent lives, human or Shifter. But it's the price that needs to be paid to keep the Meadow protected.

Time to shake it off and do my job.

I stand up, roll my shoulders, and twist my neck until it

cracks. Loosening up so I don't look as tense as I feel. There's nothing more to do now except give Hope some false reassurances and send her on her way back to Morwood.

It doesn't matter that just the thought of her leaving makes my blood run cold. I'll kiss her thoroughly and promise to see her again. But she'll hear about what I've done eventually, and then my face will haunt her nightmares instead of her daydreams.

∾

"Hello, beautiful."

I don't look up, but I sense the deep voice is meant for me. I shouldn't have slipped away when Kelsey wasn't looking, but I needed air. Staring at that closed door was infuriating. The Meadow is my home. Shifters are my people. I should be doing something, not just sitting here waiting for a human to figure it out.

He wouldn't admit the meeting had anything to do with the Meadow, but I seriously doubt the timing is a coincidence. Something happened when he met with the Elders after he returned from Morwood. Something was said, and he doesn't want to tell me about it.

A body comes close enough that I can't ignore him any longer, and my eyes travel up to the face of an Elite. As soon as our eyes meet, he smiles from ear to ear. His brown eyes are practically glowing.

"I can see why Gideon brought you home."

I look past his broad shoulders, at the entrance to Kelsey's bar, but he grips my chin and jerks my face back to look at him.

I growl a warning, already just about done with playing the helpless human. His smile spreads even wider.

"Easy there, little Shifter." Now he has my full attention.

What did Gideon tell him? He leans down until his mouth is next to my ear. "How about we step around the corner and have a chat?"

"I'm not going anywhere with you."

"That's not a smart idea. We wouldn't want anyone over-hearing that Gideon's new girlfriend is a Shifter, would we?"

"Asshole."

He laughs, then throws his heavy arm over my shoulders like we're old friends. I bite my tongue, refusing to react. "Come on. Koba's around the corner."

This must be Cade, then. Koba's Elite. I try to dig my heels in, but I can't resist without making a scene in front of the handful of humans outside the bar. And he's right, I don't want to make any trouble for Gideon.

I give up resisting, letting him pull me around the corner of the building and into a surprisingly clean alley.

Koba's at the back. I can feel him before I see him, his hulking white form barely hidden by the only dumpster. The Presence wakes the moment I make eye contact with him, and I can feel the same reverent curiosity that I picked up in Gideon's apartment.

"Koba says there's something wrong with your scent. He says you did something to him when he delivered my message to Gideon. That you fucked with his head."

"Why don't you let him speak for himself?" I growl out the words. Koba deserves to know the truth. I should have told him when I had the chance back at Gideon's flat, instead of being so worried about my own safety. I won't make that mistake again. "It's all a lie, Koba. You can take human form, you can speak for yourself, think for your-"

A hand clamps over my mouth as Cade pins me back against his solid body. I don't fight him. I know it would be pointless. Only my heartbeat gives away my fear.

"Get your fucking hands off her." Gideon's voice is a deadly promise.

Cade spins around with me still in his grasp. The movement gives me just enough wiggle room to twist as I shift, reshaping into my wolf, teeth bared and snarling.

Four men step up behind Gideon, Elite tattoos on their necks. Gideon glances over his shoulders at them.

"Easy now." Cade holds his hands up. "I think we just need to have a little honest conversation."

"Fuck off, Cade. She has nothing to do with this."

Cade laughs. "Really? Nothing to do with this?"

"You almost had us convinced, G." A dark-haired Elite speaks up, and Gideon bares his teeth when he looks back at the man. "You want us to kill Shifters, while you keep one hidden for yourself? And a fucking female at that..."

I can't help the whine that squeezes from my chest. The look on Gideon's face says there's truth in those words, but I don't understand...

"No." Gideon gives me a pleading look. "It's not like that."

"What the hell, man? Are you fucking your new dog?"

The words are barely out of Cade's mouth before Gideon's fist connects with his face. All the men draw their weapons. All aimed at Gideon, except for Cade.

He points his gun at me as he rubs his jaw, and I flatten my ears as I growl my own warning. This asshole's going to need stitches before this is over.

I don't know what's happening. I don't know why these men are here, how they knew about me, or why they're accusing Gideon of being the one who wants to harm Shifters.

Gideon raises his hands in surrender, and I want to yell at him. All I can do is bark, keeping my teeth bared and letting him know that I'm not the least bit interested in giving up.

Alpha.

The word comes to me, and I whip my head around. Koba. He's mirroring my stance, ears flat, head down, teeth bared. His eyes are locked on Cade. His bondmate.

No!

But he can't hear me. He digs his claws into the pavement as he lunges for Cade, who reacts in a blur of movement as he turns his weapon on his own Shifter. There's an explosion of sound, and searing pain rips through me as Koba's mighty body hits the ground in a heap at Cade's feet.

I don't think. I just react, as I shift back to my human form and rush to Koba's side. Thick, crimson blood stains his lush fur and spreads across the cold ground, telling me what I already know. The pain in my head disappeared as fast as it came, but the ache in my chest brings me to my knees as I wrap my arms around his motionless chest.

I look up at Cade through the blur of tears. His face is twisted in pain and shock.

"He... he was going to kill me." Cade aims the weapon at me again.

"Back off, Cade." Gideon's voice pulls my eyes away from Cade. My stomach turns to stone at the sight of a gun pressed to his temple.

"What did you have planned for her?" Cade asks. "Did you plan to turn her in, or were you aiming to use her for yourself?"

His words are senseless. Gideons looks as confused as I am, but I don't know what to trust anymore.

"I don't know what you're talking about."

"Bullshit." Cade spits on the pavement. "You had to have known they could track her when she's this close to BioSol. You can't be that stupid."

"What's he talking about, Gideon?"

"I swear I don't have a fucking clue."

Cade looks at me, his eyes as cold as the gun that's still

pointed at my head. "The signal you use to control our Shifters is trackable at close range. They picked up on it now and then over the years, but didn't have the tech to track it accurately until recently. They picked it up here last week. Followed it right up to Gideon's flat."

"I don't understand..."

"Save it. It's damn clear you can do exactly what they said you could." He nods at Koba's body, a flash of grief clouding his eyes before they turn cold again. "What I don't understand is why G thought he could play with the Elder's toy before turning you in. Pretty fucking risky for a piece of ass. Even a quality-"

"Shut the fuck up, Cade." Gideon's pure rage, his body as tense as his balled fists.

But is he angry because it's all a lie, or because he's been caught?

The Elder's know what the Presence is and they're looking for me. And Gideon knew about it? Was that the real reason he was at the Lake? Was he ever there to warn us, or just to find me? How could anyone, let alone the humans, possibly know about me?

"Doesn't matter now," Cade says. "Tranq them both."

MISTAKES

That was one hell of a bender.

I don't remember drinking, so I must have drained the fucking bar. I can't even think of a reason I would have decided to get this fucked up.

Something happened with Hope. We got in an argument, maybe? I don't fucking know. I groan as I roll to my side, feeling like a bruised sack of shit. Then things go from bad to worse.

A head of blond hair greets me. A soft, feminine scent.

Fuck.

I push myself up, my back against a wall. I'm in a small office, on a tiny cot just big enough for me and the sleeping body next to me. A small, square window high on the wall lets in a beam of early morning light.

I don't want to see this woman's face. I don't care who she is. Sliding my way down the bed, I make it halfway before the frame wobbles and creaks. The blond head turns, and blue eyes meet mine.

Holy fuck.

"Kelsey?"

My voice sounds like gravel. I swallow against sandpaper. What the fuck did I do last night?

"Hey, handsome." Her voice is smooth as silk as she slides a hand up my arm. "How did you sleep?"

I close my eyes, blocking out her, the room, the bed. I try to remember something, anything. There shouldn't be any lasting memory lapse once my Medic scrubs the last of the alcohol out of my system.

"Fuck, Kelsey. Did we..." I can't even finish the sentence.

Her breathy moan makes my heart drop into my stomach. Then she slaps me, and my eyes fly open to meet her pissed off glare.

"Seriously, Gideon? We're fully dressed... and I'm fully gay. If your man-charms didn't convert me before, I highly doubt having your drunk ass hauled to bed by your buddies will make my panties melt."

Thank fuck. I'm so relieved, I don't even care that I just made an epic fool of myself. She climbs off the bed, and I fall back onto the pillow, pressing my fingers into my temples. None of this makes sense.

"Where are we?"

"In my office, at my bar. Where I don't spend the night, because I have a perfectly comfortable bed and a warm body waiting for me at home."

I sit up again. I'm in my full tactical gear, weapons still strapped in place.

"I wasn't drinking. I wouldn't-"

Memory hits me like a bad dream.

"When did they bring me here?"

"Around midnight."

That mess in the alley went down before nine am. What the fuck did they do, stash me in a trunk for the day? Guess I missed the official task force meeting. Can't say I give a shit right about now.

"What is it, Gideon? What's going on?"

"Where's Hope?"

She sucks in a breath, wrapping her arms around herself. "I don't know... they said she took off in her wolf form. I figured that's why you were drinking..."

"Fuck!" I jump out of bed and stumble across the floor as my brain spins inside my head.

"Easy, big guy." She grabs my waist like she could actually support me if I went down. To be fair, stopping drunk men from cracking their skulls on the floor is a common enough occurrence in her job.

"If they hurt her, I swear..." I bite my tongue. I know I'd fucking kill them. Job or no job. Fuck the Protectors. Fuck the Elders.

"You really like her, don't you?"

I push away from her prying eyes, finding my feet as the last of the after-effects of whatever they hit me with wear off.

"Does she love you back?"

"Goddamnit, Kelsey. It's not like that." I want to make a joke about her getting all emotional after sleeping with me, but I can't seem to find the humor that should be there. I head for the door. "Sorry about all this. I'll make it up to you."

"I know you don't think you deserve to be loved, but you have to know Lily wasn't your fault."

I freeze with my hand on the door. What the hell is she doing?

"You don't know what you're talking about."

"I hear plenty around here. You're not my only friend from high places."

"Then you know damn well I don't deserve to be... to be with someone."

"Lily died during labor. It's rare, but it happens-"

"Back off, Kelsey."

"There was nothing you could have done. The doctors couldn't save her or the baby. It's a fucking tragedy, but it wasn't your fault."

I don't know why my hand drops from the door handle. I don't need this shit. I don't want to hear any of it. Whatever she thinks she knows, it doesn't matter.

"Don't pity me, Kelsey. You don't know the whole story."

"Tell me, then. Make me understand."

"Why?" I turn on her, raw anger surging through my veins. Lily. Hope. They both would have been better off staying clear of me. Kelsey backs up a step. Good. "Why the fuck do you think you want to hear it?"

"Because I care about you. For some damn reason I can't understand, you've managed to get under my skin. The pain in your eyes, even when you're smiling, makes my heart ache."

I don't need this right now. I just need to find Hope and get her back to the Meadow where she'll be safe.

I push out into the darkened bar. Kelsey's office opens behind the counter, and I head for the washroom to take a piss and make sure I don't look like I slept at a bar.

When I come back out, Kelsey's waiting. I make for the exit, but she intercepts with a hand on my arm.

"You deserve to move on, Gideon. You made mistakes, bad shit happened, and you've suffered for it. You can move on."

"Mistakes?" I can't stop the words from spilling out. "I guilted her into keeping a pregnancy she didn't want. We didn't even like each other. I wasn't there when she went into labor early, and I ignored her calls when they were dying on our kitchen floor."

Kelsey's eyes are brimming with tears, and it makes me want to throw a table through the fucking window.

"I heard it was a stroke."

"Yeah. Which they would have survived with the proper medical attention. I thought she was calling to bitch at me."

"She could have called an ambulance."

"She called *me*. I was selfish, and they died." I pull out of her grip and continue walking. "Save your sympathy for someone who deserves it."

GIDEON'S NAME is my first thought as awareness hits me like a kick in the ribs. Then the weight of betrayal settles in my gut. I scramble to my feet, blinking away the haze as my surroundings come into focus.

I'm in my wolf form in a small, white room that smells like bleach. One wall is metal bars, and I fight the urge to throw myself at them. To claw and bite and tear my way out. I need to be calm so I can figure this out.

On the other side of the bars, a man with a round belly slouches in a chair. His breathing is steady, his hat pulled down over his eyes.

There's a small television mounted on the wall. A news station plays with the volume low, a demure woman with red lips standing at a podium, addressing a cheering crowd as she talks about her plans and promises. Human politics.

I step up to the bars, pushing my shoulder against them, but they're every bit as sturdy as they look. I shift to human form, keeping my eyes on the sleeping man as I run my hands over the door, feeling for the latch and trying without success to open the cage.

Cage. The word brings a fresh wave of panic, and I have to fight not to lose control.

Where am I? Where's Gideon? The last image I have of him

is the moment Cade ordered the other men to tranquilize us. Gideon looked at me and the world went black. Is he here, too? Did they capture us both? But I know how unlikely that is. Humans don't get put in cages.

I sink down to the hard, polished floor, clasping my hands over my mouth as an involuntary sob tears from my chest.

The man jolts, his eyes landing on me and widening. I shift to my wolf form as he jumps to his feet. We stare at each other for a moment, my lips curled back from my teeth. A useless display considering the bars that separate us.

He reaches to press a small, orange button on the wall beside the only door in the room. A moment later, it pushes open and a gray-haired man in a white coat steps through. His short hair is sticking up at odd angles, his blue eyes bright to match the wide smile on his face.

"My god, there you are." He breathes the words like a prayer. "Those eyes. I never thought I'd see the day."

I growl, but I force my ears and tail up as I back away from the bars. You're happy to see me? Come, open the door...

"We spared no expense trying to find that man. I thought we lost you."

What is he talking about? Who does he think I am?

"Do you even know what you are?"

He watches me, waiting, and I have to look away from the intensity of the questions in his eyes.

"You don't, do you? What did he tell you?"

I look back at him, and my gaze lands on the symbol sewn into the chest of his white coat. A stylized microchip. The logo for Biological Solutions. I'm at BioSol Labs.

"Will you shift? Will you talk to me?"

I growl my response, and he nods. He licks his lips, his eyes darting from side to side as if he's trying to decide what to say next.

"Leave us," he says without looking over his shoulder.

"That's not a good idea, sir."

"It's fine. She's contained. Give me five minutes."

The first man nods, although he doesn't seem pleased with being ordered away. When the door closes behind him, the gray-haired man looks back at me.

"My name is Doctor Amos Stevenson. I'm a scientist with the Shifter program here at BioSol."

I refuse to show a reaction to his words. Why is he introducing himself like we'll shake hands and chat? The Shifter program. The people who enslave our males and murder our females.

"I started here as a researcher, and a long time ago I worked with a man named Carl Edwards."

I bristle at the sound of my father's name, my hackles rising despite my attempt to appear neutral.

"You know him, then? Is he still alive? Was he in Moridian with you? Dr. Edwards was a promising scientist, and he was my friend..."

I shake my head. Why would I expect to learn anything real from the humans here? The man tips his head in confusion, and I turn my back on him. I'm not interested in his lies.

"Is he alive? I can't imagine he would have let you out of his sight. Unless... did the bond fail? Did you break it?"

I can't stand it anymore. I don't know what this man is trying to get out of me, but if he's just trying to provoke me into shifting, it's working. I turn and grab the bars with human hands. He jumps to his feet, mouth gaping as if he's in shock at the sight of me.

"Shut up!" I growl the words through clenched teeth. "I don't know what you're talking about. I'm not who you think I am!"

He closes his mouth, his throat working in slow motion as he swallows.

"I would recognize your eyes anywhere. Their color is tied to the Alpha gene. It's as clear as a neon sign above your head." His gaze sweeps over me.

Tears sting my eyes, and I blink them away. I won't get out of this mess by acting like an animal, or by giving in to fear. "I don't know what you're talking about. Carl Edwards isn't a scientist. He's my father."

Dr. Stevenson's eyebrows nearly hit the ceiling, the genuine surprise at my words almost making me second guess my own mind.

"He worked here," I explain, "But he was a custodian. He saved my mother's life when she would have been incinerated like all the other females. He ran away to save her. They fell in love." I stand a little straighter, looking Dr. Stevenson in the eyes. "I'm a natural Shifter."

The silence is heavy as he stares back at me. More than his words, it's the pity in his eyes that has me feeling like everything I know is on the brink of collapsing.

"Has he not told you what you are?"

I step back. My heart is racing. I'm standing on the edge of something I've always known existed, but could never define. The question that's always been on the tip of my tongue.

"What am I?"

The door flies open hard enough to bang against the wall. Two armed guards walk in, along with a woman in a lab coat identical to Dr. Stevenson's.

"Let's go, Doctor." She says the command with an unmistakable tone of authority.

I grip the bars. "Wait!"

"I'm sorry, child." Dr. Stevenson doesn't look back at me as the guards move to let him out of the room.

"What am I?" I ask it again, looking from him to the woman who ordered him away.

"You're BioSol property."

Her words are ice. She steps up to the television, pressing a button to turn it off. Then she turns her back, switching off the lights as she leaves with the guards.

REALIZATIONS

*A*t least this room isn't white. I've never liked white, which is proof enough that I have no control over my animal form, considering the color of my wolf.

I bang the back of my head against the wall. One, two, three times. I'd rather be a white wolf than nothing at all. I'm nothing but an animal to these people, which is a bit ironic since they've made sure I can't shift out of my human form.

I look down at my arm, and the chemical restraint that's ensuring I don't have any hope of fighting my way out.

They brought me here through the nursery. Glass rooms with mothers and their young. Weanlings on display, waiting for a human to bond with before their time runs out.

It's so unnatural. So wrong.

Shifter embryos are imported from Centauri B, then implanted into ordinary bears, big cats, and wolves. The young are born with a genetic kill-switch. If they don't bond with a human host within three months, they die. If their human host dies, they die. Their only purpose is to serve.

But they knew me. As I walked past the cages, the older weanlings looked at me. All of them. They stared, and they put their little paws and noses on the glass. I swear I could feel their fear, their sorrow, and the tender thread of life that could be over at any moment.

The Presence responded to them. It clawed and crawled under my skin until I thought I might lose my mind.

Maybe I have.

Even now, I can hear them like an echo of my soul. If I close my eyes, they seem to be waiting for me in the Darkness. I want to go there with them, but it feels farther away than ever. I squeeze my eyes shut, trying to get there, but the stench and chill of the evil around me pulls me back.

Damon told me he wanted to burn this place to the ground. I should never have stopped him.

"How do you like your new room?"

I jump at the sound of a woman's voice. The same woman who ordered Dr. Stevenson away and left me in the dark. I turn my face away from her. Putting me in a cell with a cot and a toilet doesn't make it any less of a cage.

"My name is Dr. Marilyn Chambers. Where is Carl Edwards?"

"I don't know."

"Why were you with an Elite? What's his role in this?"

I grind my teeth. I don't want to answer her. I don't want to give her anything she could use against me or the people I love. But I also have my own questions. I desperately need answers, and after my brief encounter with Dr. Stevenson... I think this might be the place to find them.

"He... I followed him to Moridian."

"Is he working with Dr. Edwards?"

"Why do you keep calling him that? My father isn't a doctor or a-"

"How much control do you have over them?"

"I don't know what you're talking about." I stand up,

moving closer to the bars. I look her in the eyes even though her frigid expression makes me want to cower. "I don't understand what you think I am."

The woman stares back at me, and a hint of warmth seems to soften her features. Just a little. She reaches into her pocket and pulls out a key.

"Will you let me show you?"

I'm nodding before I've even considered what she could mean. I need to know. Whatever she has to say, I need to hear it.

She pulls her comm out of her other pocket and holds it up for me to see. "I have remote control of your restraint. My finger will be on the button. If you try to run or harm me in any way-"

"I won't."

"Good." She opens the door and gestures for me to step out and walk beside her.

Dr. Chambers leads the way through stark hallways and past closed doors labeled with numbers that don't seem to progress in any logical order. This part of BioSol isn't for the public, or anyone that doesn't work here.

We reach a door that's just as anonymous as the others, and she shields her hand to key in a code on the lock pad. Inside is a white room just like the one I first woke up in. In the cage are two men. One looks my age, his reddish hair shaggy around his face. The other looks to be ten or fifteen years older, with short, dark hair and a dense beard.

They're wearing jeans and t-shirts, and they sit against opposite walls. As far from each other as they can get in the small space. The older man looks at me first, his dark eyes brightening with something that looks a little too close to hope.

My name is a cruel joke, because I can't offer them a bit of it.

The younger man turns his head toward me, and his green

eyes flash with something even warmer. I look away. I've never seen these men, but I know they're Shifters even before Dr. Chambers starts to talk.

"Awakened Shifters. That's what they're calling themselves."

She steps farther into the room to sit on a chair that faces the cage. Her comm is in her hand, her finger hovering over the screen, ready to push the command that would send a heavy dose of sedative into my veins.

"Because they understand the lie now. Because as willing slaves, they didn't know who they really were. Or who they could become."

"It's a romantic thought. But it's also a dangerous one." She looks up at me, her brow creased. "I'm not lost on how gray the morality of it all is. You're sentient. Intelligent. You experience the same emotions humans do, as far as we can tell. But even if you can live without the bond, it doesn't change the fact that you wouldn't exist without it."

"I exist."

"You certainly do. But you exist because of the Shifter program. Because you were purchased, modified, and sold as any other weapon to the military. You would not be on this planet, you would not even be alive, if humans didn't make you for their own use."

I can't stop the growl that rumbles through my chest, and the men in the cage join in with warnings of their own. I take a deep breath, not wanting to cause any more trouble for them.

"What do you think would happen if I put you in that cage?"

My eyes snap to hers, my pulse pounding in my ears. The younger male pushes up to his feet.

"I'll tell you what would happen. They would be your puppets. They would do whatever you wanted of them, without you having to speak a word. Even though they don't understand the compulsion, they're waiting for you to tell them what to do."

"No... that's not... I can't..."

Even as I struggle to deny what she's saying, I look at the males as they're looking back at me. Waiting.

"Why are they here?"

She takes a deep breath, pausing long enough for me to think she won't answer. "Research," she says, like it's no big deal. "They'll be the first to try our newest project; an injectable compound that deactivates the genes responsible for shapeshifting."

I look down at her, and I'm sure the horror I feel is written all over my face. "Why would you..."

"Preventing shifting, selective shifting, bigger, stronger, more prolific... purple fur. The possibilities are limitless with unlimited funding and off-world technology."

"You're a monster."

"You really don't know, do you?" She stands up from the chair, ignoring my insult. "I worked with Carl. We discovered the Alpha gene together, and he betrayed me when he stole you from the lab and disappeared for twenty-five years."

I feel the air sucked from the room, and I wrap my arms around myself. I shake my head. "No. Why would I believe you? Why would I believe anything you say?"

"You don't need to. It won't change anything."

She leaves the room, and I take one last look at the males in the cage. "I'll help you, if I can," I whisper, but I don't wait for their reaction as I hurry to follow Marilyn down the hall.

"Tell me the rest!" I shout as I catch up, and she turns toward me with raised eyebrows and a smug smile. She has me right where she wants me, but I don't care. "I need to know what I am."

~

I DON'T KNOW if it's been hours or days. The passing of time is impossible to judge in this place. Moving from room to room, bright lights to dark; it has my internal clock doing zig zags.

I rub my arm at the crook of my elbow. Just a little blood sample, she said. A trade. They want to study me, for what reason I can't grasp. But I want information, and no price feels too high.

They took so much blood that I had to lean on a guard to make it back to my room. My cage. And do I actually believe she will tell me anything at all tomorrow, like she promised? I'm not sure if I even believe there's anything to tell.

Nothing she or Dr. Stevenson has said so far makes any sense. Father wasn't a scientist. He doesn't know a syringe from a scalpel. Not that she accused him of being an MD, but still. He's not comfortable around anything to do with the clinic, or the equipment we get from BioSol.

He carves his wood and supports my mother. He was brave when he rescued her, and he did great things in those months... but *Doctor* Edwards? It's ridiculous.

But she has to know something. The Presence, the way she described it. She thinks I'm much more capable than I am, but she's on the right track.

I almost want to laugh at the absurdity of it. My defect is defective. Isn't that just a kick while I'm down.

Does it even matter? Nothing is what I thought it was. My life was a lie. I'm a lie. But at least I'm not afraid anymore. The unknown menace of the Presence, and the Darkness waiting behind my eyes... there's nothing there that terrifies me anymore. Maybe I'm just learning not to care.

"Hope?"

I jump at the sound of a hushed voiced. Why would she

come back now? She said she was going home for the night and would be back to talk with me in the morning. Or maybe it's morning already. Maybe it was never even night... oh blazes, I'd give anything to see the sky right now. Just the thought makes my skin prickle with the urge to shift, even though this cursed restraint is still firmly in place.

"Hope, it's me, Tanner."

I'm confused for just a moment before excitement kicks in.

"Tanner!"

"Oh, my goodness, girl!"

Tanner's the bravest Shifter I know. He lives in Moridian, working night security at BioSol. He was awakened early on, about twenty years ago, but he liked being a Protector. He wanted to do more for the Meadow than just hide in it.

His Agent was a good man, and he helped Tanner get the credentials he needed for a job in security at BioSol. He's been our eyes and ears there ever since, and he's the reason we can get supplies and equipment without anyone ever noticing. Now, there are four Shifters living as humans and working at BioSol, but he's the one who has the most reach.

"How did you manage to get yourself here?" His fingers fly over the keypad for the cage lock. "I could hardly believe my eyes when I got to work this evening."

"I'm sorry. I was... I was stupid. I shouldn't have..."

"Shhh, stop that now. It's not your fault. I'm going to get you out of here and you high-tail it right back to the Meadow, okay?"

He swings the door open, but even as my heart skips a beat at the thought of freedom, I can't move. This isn't a prison, even if it feels like it is. It's a lab. They want to learn something from me, and I have things I want to learn from them... If Tanner can get me out this easily tonight, he can get me out just as easily another night. After I find out what Dr. Chambers has to say.

"Come on, girl. Your safe."

"You'll get in trouble."

"Don't you worry about that. I've been a loyal employee here for two decades. If they haven't caught me swiping stuff yet, I doubt tonight will be the night. I know my way around these security systems like you know your way around a body, Doctor Hope."

"I might learn something here... something that could help the Meadow..." It's not really a lie. If I learn what the Presence is, I'll know if it's something that can help the Meadow, or hurt it.

Tanner gives me a look that says he knows I'm keeping something from him. I know he won't pry.

"There was an Elite here looking for you earlier today."

That makes me get to my feet. "Gideon?"

Tanner raises an eyebrow, the corner of his mouth twitching.

"He was here?"

"Sure was. I saw the security footage myself. I take it you know him?"

"Yeah, he's on our side." My statement doesn't sound so confident. Is Gideon on our side? I can't make any sense out of what I heard in the alley. "At least, I think he is."

You want us to kill Shifters... What did that even mean? Were they just trying to provoke Gideon? Those men were Elites. It doesn't make sense.

I cover my face with my hands, sure that Tanner can see everything I feel. "I don't know who to trust anymore."

"It's okay, girl." His voice is low and soothing. "I'm sure he's one of the good ones. I haven't seen him around here in a few years. Not since before he lost his wife."

That statement snaps me right out of my wallowing.

"Poor thing. And the baby, too. Such a sad thing to happen to such a sweet, young family."

Tanner shakes his head, his lips pressed into a thin line to match the creases in his forehead. I can't breathe. The weight on my chest is far too heavy.

I don't know what's real. I don't know what to think about Gideon after what I saw in that alley. A chill washes over me, and I feel wrong even asking, but I have to know. "How did she... how did they..." I clear my throat, and I can't look at him as I force out the question. "How did his wife and child die?"

"She had a stroke. It was over a month before she was due, if I remember correctly. I heard they likely would have survived, but she was alone when it happened. By the time he found her, it was too late for both of them."

I squeeze my eyes shut as tears escape down my cheeks. I'd be affected even if this were a story about a complete stranger. But picturing Gideon... imagining him finding his family like that... I can't even comprehend the pain. The guilt he must live with.

I flash back to the moments we had. The moments when he was opening up, sharing his body and his heart. I'm torn between the desire to comfort him, to show him he deserves to be loved... and the sinking feeling that he's more foe than friend.

I hear a faint *click* as the pressure from the chemical restraint eases.

I feel so alone. I close my eyes, letting the Darkness surround me. I sink farther than I ever have, giving in to the vacuum as my troubles seem to fade away. I'm completely alone.

Or maybe not...

I can feel Tanner. Not just his hand on my shoulder and his

warmth at my side. I can feel his mind. I can feel those two newly awakened males, like warm patches of sunlight. The young in the nursery. Plus, three, no, four others in the lab.

The Presence tingles along my spine, spreading through my body as my awareness seems to radiate from where I stand, expanding outward. The bright spots of Shifters shine throughout Moridian, Solar One, the brilliant beacon of the Meadow like a blazing campfire in the night.

I'm not alone. Not as long as we survive.

I'm on the edge of something, of understanding, it's just within my grasp and I reach for it with an open palm...

"Hope!" Tanner's voice shatters the illusion, and I'm pulled away from *We*, back to me. I feel myself crumble as the cold edges of the lab surround me again.

"I need to go home."

RETURN

$\mathcal{I}$'m doing the right thing.

That certainty keeps my paws pounding into the earth as I weave through the trees toward the Meadow, even though my heart aches at the unanswered questions I'm leaving behind.

I still don't understand it all. I still can't define it or explain what I feel in any words that make sense. But I know without a doubt the Presence isn't something I need to fight. It's real, it's alive, but it's no parasite or tumor to be found and cut out. It's me. It's them. It's *We*.

The words don't make sense.

But the feeling does.

I'm way past exhausted when I burst from the forest into the gardens of the Meadow, and my face hits the dirt as my legs give out. I lay where I land, heaving and gulping greedy breaths.

It's a drizzly night, and the waning moon casts its misty glow over everything. No one seems to have heard me arrive, and that makes anger flare in my belly. We need to protect this place better... someone should have noticed my approach long before I reached this point.

The heavy thud of something hitting the ground at my flank has me scrambling to my feet. My legs are like rubber, and I sway like a newborn fawn. My fear fades instantly, as I see Tarek's bulky form crouched near me.

I guess I wasn't so unnoticed, after all.

"Welcome back." His emerald eyes are bright in the moonlight. "Are you running away from something, or toward something?"

"Maybe a little of both." I admit, my abused muscles protesting the shift.

"Gideon okay?"

Heat rises in my cheeks at the sound of his name in Tarek's deep voice. His concern for the man who used to be his bondmate is rare. There seems to be no resentment, only friendship.

"I don't know." My answer earns a thick growl from Tarek, and I can see his skin ripple with the urge to shift. "He's involved with something. I don't know if he's with us anymore."

"What do you mean?" He steps closer to me, his eyes darkening.

I tell him everything that happened in the alley. Everything I heard. When I'm done, the heavy mist is clinging to our hair and making our clothes fit like a second skin.

"Gideon wouldn't turn against us."

"Then why is he still there? Why is he still living in that city and carrying that title?"

"Because he can do more from the inside. He can work for change in ways we can't."

"Does he, though? Has he?"

"I trust him."

Gideon's own words come to mind; '*That is who I am,*

Hope. I use people to get what I want.' He all but told me himself. No matter how much he cares, or how much he wants to help, he will always put himself and his career first.

"What do you want me to do?" Tarek's question makes me sway on my feet. Who am I to tell him what to do?

Alpha. My eyes widen at the same moment Tarek's do, as we both feel the weight of that word at the same instant.

"Find him. Make sure he's okay, but don't trust him."

Tarek nods, no hesitation in his movements as he pushes backward and up, his body shifting fluidly from his human form to the mighty dragon. With a few strong pumps of his wings, he takes off toward Moridian.

I don't hesitate either, as I turn my back to the forest and head into the little village of tents and freshly built cabins.

I NEVER WASTED a bit of food when Tarek lived here. With the appetite of a grizzly, there was no such thing as leftovers. Thank fuck for delivery services, because if I'd had to cook for him, he would have starved to death within the first week.

I shove the dish of cold eggs and sausage into the fridge, telling myself I'll reheat it tomorrow.

It's five a.m., and I've already spent two hours in the gym, showered, cooked, eaten and cleaned up breakfast.

I'm just trying to keep busy until the sun rises and I can get to work. Anything to keep my mind off the guilt that's churning in my gut. Not that it's an unfamiliar emotion.

I should never have gotten Hope wrapped up in all of this. I could have refused to help her get out of Morwood. I certainly should never have brought her home.

Just another entry in the long list of ways I've royally fucked shit up in my life.

What's the point? What's the point of any of this? I can't even come up with an answer. All I can see is her face. She was my last chance at something real.

My last hope.

After I left Kelsey's, I went straight to BioSol. I was so sure I'd be able to get to her. Sure I'd walk in there, flash my credentials, and walk out with her safe and sound. It was a stupid thought. Even an Elite doesn't have clearance inside those walls.

Short of taking a hostage, which definitely crossed my mind as a viable solution, there was no way I was getting any information out of them or even getting past the front desk.

The Elders blew me off when I requested clearance, which shouldn't surprise me. Whatever Cade was on to, and whatever role Hope plays in it, the Elders are deliberately keeping me out of it.

I need someone on my side. Someone who's still on the Elder's good side. As much as I hate the man after what went down, Cade is my best option. I need to know what he knows, and I need him to understand what's at stake.

Kelsey couldn't have been more wrong about me.

Not just about Lily. I didn't cause the stroke that took them, but the fact remains that if it weren't for me being selfish and immature, she would never have gotten pregnant. She definitely wouldn't have stayed pregnant.

Kelsey's speech reminded me of one thing. Her affection for someone like me. Her compassion for a species most people don't even attempt to understand. She reminds me that there are good people in the world.

I'm not one of them. I use people to get what I need. I used Lily. Tarek. Whisper. Hell, even my rank as an Elite Protector... it's never been about protecting anything. It's only ever been about the rank, the title, the accomplishments. The pay check.

Not anymore. It's time I used my abilities for something more. For her. Not to earn her love or some romantic shit like that. Fuck that. By the time I'm done, love will be the last thing she feels for me.

I'll protect her, and the Meadow, by doing what needs to be done.

The rap of knuckles against glass makes me realize I'm still staring into the fridge. I swing it closed, my mood lightening instantly at the sight of Tarek on my balcony.

Welcome home, brother, I say through our Link.

I slide the door open and slap a hand against his over-muscled shoulder. I'm still a little jealous of his bulk. Fucker had to outdo me, which shouldn't be a surprise considering he always got a kick out of how many hours I put into the gym.

He returns the gesture with a friendly punch that makes me stifle a groan. He heads for the fridge, and in a moment my left-over breakfast is spinning in the microwave.

"What brings you here?"

"Hope sent me."

I swear my heart stops beating. "Hope?"

"Yep." He takes the food out of the microwave, grabbing a carton of orange juice before settling down at the table. "You must have made quite an impression. She wanted me to make sure you're okay."

Fuck, there's not enough oxygen in the room. Tarek eyes me as he eats.

"She's safe? Where is she?" I try not to sound like I'm desperate for confirmation. Just curious. Not holding my breath until he say's the words.

"She's good. Arrived back at the Meadow during the night. Ran herself into the ground trying to make good time."

"What happened to her? How did she..." What's the point of

knowing the details? It won't change anything. "Never mind. I'm just glad she's back where she belongs."

"She was worried about you."

He's fishing for details, but I don't plan to give him any. She was worried about me. Hell, she was the one in danger. She was the one with too much to lose.

I shake my head, clearing my thoughts. Whatever happened between Hope and I, whatever could have happened, it's in the past.

"Go back. Tell her I'm fine and she needs to stay in the Meadow. The city's not safe. Not for any of you."

Tarek narrows his eyes as he sets his fork down on an empty plate. "What's going down? Something I need to know?"

"Nothing you won't know soon enough. Just get back there and keep her safe. Keep yourself safe."

He stands, leaving his dishes on the table as he walks over to me. "I'm not pushing, because I trust your judgment. But I don't appreciate being a fucking message boy in a lover's quarrel."

"It's not like that."

"Whatever, brother. I'm going." He walks to the balcony, but pauses with his hand on the door. "There's something different about her."

"I know."

"No, I mean… It's like she gets in my head. I'm not even sure what I'm talking about. It's just a feeling."

All I can do is nod. I don't enjoy lying to Tarek, even by omission. But what Hope chooses to tell him is her business.

A new idea enters my mind. "Before you head back, can you meet me at the edge at eight thirty?"

"*W*hat am I?"

The question's getting easier to ask every time. I know it has an answer, and once I have the full story, everything's going to change.

"Hope, please. Stop."

Mother actually seemed relieved to see me, after the initial shock of being woken up in the small hours of the morning. She even hugged me, wet clothes and all, which is something she hasn't done since I was a child.

The affection didn't last long. As soon as I started asking questions they didn't want to answer, she was right back to her usual self.

"This isn't nonsense, Mother. I deserve to know what I am. I deserve the truth, for once."

"You are our daughter. You are the first natural Shifter."

"Should I go back to BioSol and talk with Dr. Chambers?"

Father's on his feet in an instant, anger flashing in his eyes. "What are you talking about?"

"Marilyn was more than happy to chat with me. So was

Amos." Even as I deliver the thinly veiled accusation, I still can't believe their claims were true.

"You were at BioSol?" Mother's eyes are dark as she backs away until she can sit on the edge of her bed.

"I could have stayed there and gotten more answers, but I came back because protecting the Meadow is the most important thing. It's all I care about. But I need to know what I am... I need to know who I am. And if you won't tell me everything now, I'm going back."

I stare at Mother, imploring her to talk, but all she does is stare at Father. He looks to me with a chill in his eyes that makes me feel like I'm talking to a stranger. I know the answer to my next question before I even ask.

"Were you a custodian at BioSol?"

"No."

"Carl!" Mother shushes him, but one look has her lowering her eyes.

"Tell me."

"I was a geneticist. I studied Shifter DNA."

"Who else knows this?"

"No one. Only your mother."

"Why did you lie?"

His eyes flash down for a moment before he looks back at me. "Because I stole something."

Dread settles in my belly. "What did you steal?"

Mother chokes on a sob as I blink back tears.

"You."

Father's admission hits me like a kick in the chest. I can't speak for a few agonizing moments. "Are you my parents?"

"Yes! We raised you. Your mother carried you. Gave birth to you. You are our daughter."

"But there's nothing natural about me, is there?"

Mother sinks to the floor, her face buried in her hands.

Father rubs a palm over his graying beard, his eyes focusing on something only he can see.

"Marilyn and I were tasked with inspecting the incoming Shifter embryos, and I discovered a new gene. Something latent. Ancient. We took it up the chain, telling them what we thought it could mean. They said we weren't qualified to be conducting that level of research, and likely didn't know what we were looking at."

He starts to pace, and I step back to give him room.

"We continued under the radar, developing and testing our theory. Activating the gene sequence in males led to unviable embryos every time. But when we tested it on female embryos, it seemed to work.

Marilyn wanted to turn in our research. Prove our theory was valid and get the recognition and funding we deserved. But she couldn't see the big picture. If what we theorized was true, we were on the cusp of something that could change everything about the Shifter program.

All she cared about was the money. She didn't care that the research would be taken out of our hands and given to more senior geneticists."

He looks at me for the first time since he started talking. "I made a decision. I took the altered embryos and a female pup, and I disappeared. When she was mature enough, I implanted your mother with the embryos. Ten of them. You were the only one that survived to term."

I'm a science experiment. I'm...

"What does the gene do?"

Father swallows, licking his lips as his eyes dart from me, to Mother, to the exit. He's afraid.

"I called it the Alpha gene. My theory is that in your natural form, Shifters behave much like bees, or ants. With a queen connecting them all. A hive mind."

I don't know what to say. It's too much for me to process all at once. My entire life, my identity... everything I thought I was is being rearranged into something I don't understand.

"Do you feel it, Hope? Do you feel anything at all?"

He's looking at me with intense curiosity. Like a scientist. I wrap my arms around my waist, feeling like the experiment I really am.

"I don't know," I lie.

"You displayed natural leadership tendencies, and you've always cared more about others than yourself. Saying no to you has always been impossible." He laughs at that, as if replaying some fond memories. "We learned early on that if we wanted you to do something, we had to convince you it was your idea."

"We never meant to hurt you." Mother is standing now, her eyes puffy and red from crying.

"You used me." I look between the two of them, struggling to dissolve the fake love story they've fed me, to see the truth of the people in front of me. "He used you. He saved you from the lab because he needed you to incubate his science project. He never loved you."

"Stop, Hope. You can't possibly understand."

"I'll never understand. I don't think I even want to try. Your experiment is over. All that matters now is protecting the Meadow."

"You are the Meadow." Mother says, echoing the words she spoke before I left for Moridian.

"Why did you even start this? If all you cared about was your experiment, why involve so many people?"

Father laughs. "We didn't. We tried to keep to ourselves, but once you were born, they were drawn to you. They weren't aware it was you they were seeking, but they kept coming. We realized you were compelling the Shifters to awaken, but even after we moved into the forest, more kept finding us."

"Don't go back to BioSol." Mother reaches for me, but I retreat from her hands. The wounded look on her face only lasts a moment, as she steels herself with a cool expression that's much closer to the one I'm used to. "They'll want to use you. Sell you to the highest bidder."

"And what's your intentions, then? Weren't you planning to sell me as well?"

"Never." Father's voice sounds so sincere, I want to believe it. "I wanted to prove my theory and take credit for my discovery. My notes, my research... the data alone would... I would never let them take you."

Maybe that's true, but it's little comfort now. His data would only be used to experiment on more Shifters. Make more like me to be raised in captivity.

I STRIDE into HQ as casually as any other morning. Cade waits for me in the lobby, leaning against a pillar and scrolling his comm while he sips from a takeout cup.

Just the sight of him makes my blood boil. I want to beat him for what he did to me, and to Hope. I don't trust him for a second, but I need him. He was in the lead that night, and after the way things went down with Koba, I'm counting on him being in a frame of mind to listen.

He looks up at me as I approach, a friendly smile to match my own. I asked him to meet me here, so he'd know I just want to talk.

As much as I'd like to greet him with a fist to his face, that wouldn't help me get what I need. And truthfully, if I put aside the personal aspect, I get it. I've followed orders far shadier. I've got no right to judge him for doing his job.

"Thanks for meeting me."

He nods, but his eyes are sharp as he looks for clues in my expression as to the real reason we're here. "What's up?

There's no one near us, but I step close enough that he sets his coffee down and widens his stance. "Did Koba ever take human form?"

His eyebrows raise at the question, then lower as he considers me with narrowed eyes. He does a quick scan of our surroundings before responding in a hushed voice. "Of course not. What the fuck are you on about?"

"You weren't surprised when Hope was in human form."

"Hope? I didn't know her name." He reaches a hand up and scrubs it through his short hair. "Look man, for what it's worth, I'm sorry about all that. My orders were simple and need-to-know. I didn't know what to believe. And then Koba. I don't know, man. I'm not proud of how that went down. Orders are orders, right?"

"Orders are orders." I tip my head toward the door. "Let's walk."

He nods, grabbing his drink for a last swig before chucking it into the trash. It's still half full by the sound of it. He must think it's a wise idea to keep his hands free for this conversation.

When we exit into the glaring morning light, I don't waste any time getting down to it.

"The reason we're told Shifters can't take human form is because when they do, they break the bond and become independent. They don't go insane, they don't self-destruct... they're just people. The way they were meant to be. The Centaurians created the bond to turn them into slaves."

He's quiet as we keep moving at a casual pace along the sidewalk. Even though it's busy this time of day, our tactical gear and tats clear a path wherever we go. Perks of the job, I guess.

"How do you know this?"

"Damon told me."

"Damon?" He gives me a sideways look that says he recognizes the name, but can't place it.

"Whisper's Shifter. He walked up to me, man-to-man, and told me how it is."

"Shit."

"Yep. Tarek shifted after that. He's not *my* Shifter anymore, but I'm proud to call him a friend."

Cade stops walking, and I turn to face him.

"Are you fucking with me?"

"No. I'm taking a risk because I think you'll do what's right if you're given the chance." His jaw clenches, something flashing in his eyes for half a second before he resumes walking. "Hope was born in Morwood, in a community of Shifters."

He listens as I tell him everything I know. I don't give him the location of the Meadow, or any information he could use to find them, but I lay everything else out. By the time I'm done, we're at the empty lot at the edge of the Solar.

"That's a lot of information to take in, G."

"Question is, what are you going to do with it?"

"What are you asking me to do with it?"

"They've tasked us with exterminating an intelligent species. You can try to think of them as animals, but they're just people. Different from us in some ways, same as any new race we discover out there. But still just people."

A gust of air announces Tarek's arrival, right on cue, as he swoops up from below the edge. His favorite surprise entrance. Cade holds his ground as the huge, scaled dragon settles to the ground a mere ten feet from us.

"Show him," I say as Tarek leans down to look at Cade with one wide, green eye.

He snaps his gaze to me. *You serious?*

Trust me.

Tarek hesitates. For a second I'm worried he might just bail, but then his body shakes and contracts down into his human form.

"Holy fuck," Cade says on an exhale, his tone matching his awestruck expression.

I breathe a sigh of relief. Telling him was the move that needed to be made, but there's a whole list of ways this could have gone south.

"I take it Gideon filled you in on how things are?"

"Yeah. I guess he did."

"Where's Koba?"

Cade's face goes pale. I'm sure he was already suffering after how that went down, but with this new information...

"He's gone," I say as Cade turns away. "It was a fucked up scenario. His instinct was to defend Hope. We all had our own agendas, when we should have been working together."

Cade turns back to look at us, and when I meet his eyes he nods. "It won't happen again."

"No, it won't," I agree. "Thanks for sticking around, Tarek."

Anytime, Brother.

Cade and I both watch as Tarek shifts and takes off toward the coast. As usual, he'll head out far over the water before swapping to a bird form and looping back toward Morwood.

"Now what?" Cade asks.

"Now, you put in a request for the tools we need to do our job. And make sure it's just the two of us going into BioSol."

He just stares at me like he's waiting for the punch line.

I wish there was one.

KISS ME

he afternoon light filters through the canvas of my tent, but I can't convince myself to crawl off the cot. I don't know what to do next. I feel like everything around me is fake, yet I'm the biggest fakery of it all.

I should check in with Brom, but the thought of returning to the clinic seems wrong somehow. So much has changed since I left. I've changed. I don't want to see anybody.

I was so sure coming back here was the answer. The moment I recognized that the Presence was meant to connect us, not hurt us, I knew I needed to be here with my people. But whatever euphoria came over me then, it sure disappeared fast after talking to my parents.

The Alpha gene. Like bees or ants. Is that what we are? Insects? I imagine an alien planet where Shifters live like colonies of ants. Could that be our true form?

I close my eyes, focusing on the Presence. We. The moment I think the word, it consumes me.

Awareness expands out from my body like a shockwave. Damon, River, Mother, my brothers, Brom, Sadie… I feel them all. Sparks in the Darkness. Mile by mile, far beyond the

Meadow. I soar above and through it with ease, until I collide with a flare of blue light.

I'm thrown back into my body, gasping for breath as I land on my hands and knees. What the heck was that?

It felt like hitting a wall. Like something was rushing toward me as fast as I was rushing toward it.

It can't be...

I push up to my feet, stumbling out of the tent and directly into River.

"Oh!" She squeals as we grasp onto each other to keep from falling. "Hope! Are you okay?"

"River... I... Who told you I was back?"

"No one. I just had a feeling you might be. Where were you?"

I look to my left, down the path. My oldest brother strides toward us, his usual mischievous grin intact.

"Hey, Hopeless." He throws a playful punch at my shoulder.

"Hey, Ben. Did Mother tell you I was back?"

"No, I just thought I'd check. It was weird without you around."

Something's changed. They sense the connection now, even if they don't realize what it is. Over Ben's shoulder, I see Luke on his way.

"Everything's fine. I've gotta go." I give River's arm a squeeze, then take off over the beaten paths as fast as I can.

I don't even have to think about it; I know where Damon is as surely as I know where my own two feet are without looking down. He's a part of me. They all are.

When I reach him, I'm relieved to find Whisper at his side. She's the one I need to see, but I can't sense her location like I can with Shifters.

"Whisper!" I shout her name as I reach them, and they both look at me with surprise that melts into wide smiles.

"Hey!"

"I need to talk to you," I say as I catch my breath from the sudden sprint. "Both of you."

"Okay, sure." Whisper's smile fades.

"Let's go somewhere a little quieter." I glance around, the usually indifferent faces now seeming to be watching my every move.

I hurry them to the edge of the Meadow, out of earshot of even the most sensitive Shifter ears. I tell them about the alley and the strange confrontation between Gideon and his fellow Elites. I tell them about BioSol and my conversations with Dr. Stevenson and Dr. Chambers. I tell them about my parent's confessions.

"That's incredible, Hope." Whisper seems amazed with everything I've said.

"I don't know if any of it's real, or if it's just more lies. I only know the way I feel, and the way I can connect. River and Ben, they were there to meet me when I came out of my tent, like they'd sensed my presence."

"It makes perfect sense."

Damon's confident acceptance is so unexpected, I don't know what to say.

"I was comfortable around you right from the start. Even when I didn't know if this place was safe, I still felt compelled to trust you. When I came back, I just wanted to awaken Shifters and destroy the lab. But you... I felt connected to you. I cared about you more than I've ever cared about someone other than Whisper. I wanted to protect you, and I wanted to be near you."

I know I'm blushing, and when I peek up at Whisper her brow is knitted in concentration.

"It's not just you, is it?" she asks Damon, and he shakes his head.

"It's definitely not just me. Everyone here talks about you with affection or admiration. Even Luke, as much of an asshole as he is, he's only ever trying to protect you."

"You said the gene they activated was something ancient. It's leftover from a time in Shifter history when having an Alpha that could connect with everyone was necessary for survival."

"It makes us sound like insects."

"You're definitely not insects. If that's how you lived on your native planet, there must have been an evolutionary advantage."

"There's something I'm missing. I just can't put my finger on it."

"Wouldn't an Alpha, the way your describing it, make it easier for Shifters to work together and form a community?"

"Sure, if I can learn to control it. If I could use it to communicate, I think it would work over large distances. That doesn't seem like something humans would want to encourage."

"So, there's something else we're missing. Something they can use to their advantage."

"There has to be. That's what I need to find out before I get any stronger. I don't want to be the weak spot, or the one that ends up bringing more danger here. I need to go back."

"Back to BioSol?"

"Yes. I felt something, or someone. I don't know for sure, but I think there might be another like me. I felt her... at least I think I did."

"Do you think your father's old partner kept working on it after he left?"

"I don't think she could have just let it go. She wanted to tell me more, I just didn't trust her. I still don't, but now that I know the claims she made about my father were true… I should have stayed to hear the rest."

"It's too dangerous. They won't stop at just taking blood samples. They'll want to dissect you."

"Maybe. But does that even matter? There's more to this. If there's any chance I might be a danger to the Meadow, I need to know. And I need to see her... the other..." I can't say the word. It doesn't feel right on my tongue.

"Alpha." Damon finishes my thought, and even though I want to shake my head in denial, I watch his face as the idea sinks in and he seems to relax into it. "You can't go back there. It's too dangerous."

"It doesn't matter."

"It does. You're not dangerous. You're not a threat to Shifters."

Whisper is nodding her agreement. They're not seeing the side of it that scares me the most. I haven't tried this before, and when Marilyn said it, I didn't really believe her...

"Kiss me, Damon."

Whisper sucks in a breath as Damon's expression turns to stone. I concentrate on the We, and it responds like it was ready and waiting. When it tingles at the back of my eyes, I focus only on Damon.

"Kiss me."

This time he doesn't hesitate. He leans into me so abruptly, I almost fail to dodge him in time. I pull away, shoving the Presence down as Damon stumbles on his feet.

Whisper's face is pale, both hands covering her mouth. I can't bring myself to look at Damon, though I can imagine the surprise and embarrassment on his face.

"I could be dangerous."

Whisper nods. I know she won't make excuses just to keep me safe. She knows what it takes to put your life at risk to save many more.

"I need to go back there."

"I'll help you figure out a plan."

"Thank you."

I look over at Damon, but his expression is guarded. "I'm sorry, I needed you to understand."

"It's just strange. It reminded me of my bond with Whisper. I felt compelled to do what you said, like it made perfect sense."

"The bond they manufactured between Agent and Shifter is based on an ability that was already there."

"I don't want that ability. How can you trust anything you think or feel around me?"

"I know you. You wouldn't use it against anyone."

"Do you know that for sure? Or do you just feel that way because I want you to?"

Damon's face pales, and I want to scream. It's not fair. How can I ever know if someone means what they say, or if they're agreeing with me because of a genetic predisposition?

"I feel the same way, Hope. And you don't have any sway over me."

I let out a long breath. "Yeah, I suppose. Thanks, Whisper."

She pulls me in for a tight hug. A moment later, Damon's strong arms wrap around us both. I can't stop the tears that spill down my cheeks.

SHE'S YOU

It's a little anticlimactic as I walk through the wide front gates of BioSol. No armed guards wait to detain me the moment I'm within their reach. No one in a white lab coat comes rushing out the front door. After the method they used to get me here the first time, I expected something more.

The parking lot's packed, even though it's only mid-morning. A man exits the building, the automatic doors sliding closed behind him as he clutches his hat and coat against the crisp breeze. A blue car pulls up, and he hurries into the passenger seat.

I attempt to tame my hair into an elastic while I cross the smooth pavement. The doors slide open as I force deep breaths despite my chest feeling too small for my lungs.

The reception area is as congested as the lot. I take a number and find an empty chair between a tall, thin man with a kind smile and an elderly woman wearing more jewelry than I've ever seen on one person.

I try to stifle my nerves by listening to the conversations around me. An older man talking on his comm about a business decision. A mother corralling an active toddler while wearing her sleeping baby. A young couple, leaning together as they talk about their hopes for conceiving. It's comforting to remember that this place is far more than just the Shifter program.

BioSol is the umbrella for handling all the tech that comes from Centauri B. There are military applications, including the Shifter program and other weapons. There's also the Solars, teleports, implant tech, and a ton of medical advancements. Almost half this place is clinic space, using the off-world knowledge and equipment to treat everything from infertility to genetic diseases.

For a price, of course. Nothing from Centauri is cheap. In fact, most of the tech is inaccessible to the average person, and it's only created an even bigger gap between the poor lower class and the wealthy upper class.

My number's called, and I step up to a friendly smile from the man behind the counter.

"Hello there." He does a double-take when he looks up at my eyes. "Welcome to Biological Solutions. What can we help you with today?"

"I'm here to see Dr. Marilyn Chambers."

"What time is your appointment?" His fingers fly across a keyboard.

"I don't have one." He looks up at me with an almost comically raised eyebrow. "Can you just tell her that Hope is here? I'll wait as long as it takes, but I promise you she'll want to see me."

He smiles again and gives me a nod. "Okay, Hope. I'll make sure she gets the message."

"Thank you."

I move away from the counter so the next person can move up. As soon as I sit back in my stiff chair, Dr. Chambers pushes through a door to the left of the reception desk. She scans the room and when her eyes settle on me, they widen as if she didn't believe the message she received.

I jump up and approach her, wanting to make it clear that I'm here of my own free will. "Good morning, Dr. Chambers."

"Hope." She glances around at the other people in the waiting area. Her tone is light, as if she might be suggesting a coffee and chat. Her rigid posture and stiff smile are anything but casual. "Would you like to come with me?"

"WHATEVER ROMANTIC NOTIONS you have about it, the fact remains that you were created to control. As far as your dear parents whom you speak so highly of? I would hazard to guess that your mother was distant, your father kind."

Marilyn looks at me for confirmation, but I try to give her nothing. She might be right, but it's hardly more than a lucky guess. She nods as if I've confirmed her suspicions.

"Carl wouldn't have wanted you to get too close to her for fear that you would bond with her. I bet he was always affectionate. He was either on your side, or stayed quiet while your mother played the role of disciplinarian."

"That doesn't prove anything."

She laughs that ironic chuckle of someone who thinks they know something you don't.

"Think about it, Hope. We anticipated that the gene would trigger at maturity, which should have been six months of age. But you didn't bond like other Shifters do, you survived and grew at a natural pace. He couldn't have anticipated that outcome. They must have tried to prevent you from forming deep connections, particularly romantic connections, for fear it would trigger you to bond."

"It still doesn't fit. What good could an Alpha Shifter be for humans? Keeping us divided is what makes us weak. Why would you want to give us a way to connect?"

"Think about it." She says again, and I want to pull my hair out. I am thinking about it. It's all I've been thinking about. "The Shifter embryos we receive from Centauri B require a bond with a higher life form. That bond gives a measure of control. Not over specific actions, but more of an overall compulsion to serve and obey. It ties the Shifter's life to their bondmates life, giving the Shifter even more incentive to protect them. It's a perfect symbiosis. Now, imagine combining that with the Alpha gene."

Oh, blazes. Goosebumps prickle across my skin as the obvious answer settles into place. "If I can control all the Shifters..."

"Yes. Now you're getting it."

"Whoever I bond with controls them through me."

The realization spreads like ice in my veins. I lean my back against the cold, white wall as I let it sink in.

"Exactly. Carl must have initially hoped you would bond with him. That would make him a critical part of the project, and he could have returned to the lab as a valuable asset. When you didn't bond, he would have suspected it would take a romantic connection to cement the bond... that's what I would have assumed at that point." She crosses her arms in front of her chest, her brows furrowed as she considers my life like the science experiment it is. "Have you ever had an intimate relationship? Sex, or love?"

I scoff at that, leaving her to interpret it however she likes.

Sex obviously never triggered it. As far as romantic love goes... I might not have slept with Gideon, but the way I felt with him... no, love doesn't trigger it either.

Maybe it's the combination of love and sex? Mixing the physical act with the emotions in some magical connection.

Sounds like a lame romance novel where the hero can instantly cure all the heroine's problems with his penis.

My father and Marilyn are just guessing. They have no clue why I didn't bond like every other lab Shifter. But they need to figure it out, because without that piece of the puzzle, this whole experiment is useless.

Even after all this new knowledge, one fact remains; I'm defective. I choke on a laugh at that thought, because me being defective is the only thing that's stopped them from using me for my intended purpose. And the possibility of that purpose being fulfilled makes me wish I'd never been born.

"I'm a weapon."

That's the gist of it. All Shifters are; created here and paired with Protectors to fight whatever fights their masters deem necessary. But I've always been apart from that. I was supposed to be a natural Shifter, yet I'm the deadliest weapon of all.

"Yes, essentially." Marilyn confirms my statement, and she almost sounds sympathetic.

I look up at her, my stomach contents staying in place by sheer force of will. "Aren't you afraid of me?"

She laughs, but there's a stiffness to the sound. "No, Hope. You don't have a violent bone in your body. You're a nurturer. A connector. You were never meant to be violent, only to be a conduit."

"Right." Like that makes it any better.

"It's not as if the Elders would head off to war with an army of Shifters. It's just a tool to have on hand. We're a small planet in a big cosmos. To call on the Shifters as a unified force if we ever needed to defend-"

"You're a scientist. Not a soldier or a politician. How can you possibly think you know what the Elders would do with such a *tool*?"

"Look, Hope. To be clear, it doesn't matter to me either

way. I'm not here to be the judge of good and evil. I'm here for the science."

She starts walking. My legs are weak under the weight of all I've learned, but I will myself to push off the wall and keep pace at her side.

"Where are we going?"

"I have something to show you."

"Is it her?"

Marilyn stops, turning to look at me. "How do you know about her?"

"I felt her. Who is she?"

Marilyn licks her lips, her eyes moving from side to side until she finally seems to settle on an answer. "She's you. Or, who you would have been if you'd been raised here. At least, that's my theory. Genetically speaking, you're the same. As you'll see, there are some obvious differences."

I knew the moment I connected with her she wasn't just another Shifter. She was aware and searching. Like me. But that can't be right... can there be two Alphas?

"Did she bond?"

"At first, yes. She bonded with me and experienced the accelerated growth that all lab Shifters do. Once her maturity matched mine, the bond faded. We assumed she would die. Instead, she shut down in other ways. She became non-verbal and prone to sudden aggression."

"She wasn't meant to be raised here. She was meant to be free. With other Shifter's."

"Perhaps. Nevertheless, we're on the verge of a break-through. I've been attempting to stimulate the bond through artificial means, and my last attempt was encouraging."

"How are you-"

"It doesn't matter how. That's not something I can share with you. But during my last trial, I felt something. It was a tingle, almost like the sensation of a limb falling asleep. It traveled up my spine in the strangest way. I know it means I'm close."

I know that feeling well, but I don't plan to tell her just how close she is.

If Marilyn bonds with this other Alpha, she'll have control over all Shifters. Will I even be able to help them? Can we both share the connection, or would it disconnect me from them? As much as I don't want this burden, I can't imagine losing it now.

We enter a stark hallway lined with more numbered doors, each with a small window beside it. Marilyn gestures to the fourth on the left, and I follow her lead. I peer through the glass, and my hands start to shake.

～

"SHE LOOKS LIKE ME."

"Yes, she does."

The woman on the other side of the one-way glass is nothing like I imagined. When I connected with that blue point of light; that flame in the Darkness... I don't know what I thought I would find, but it wasn't this.

She's an older version of me. Same build, same hair, same face. When she glances up at the window that looks like a mirror on her side, I see my own eyes staring at me.

"What's her name?"

"Violet. She prefers Vi."

Vi is sitting at a small desk, sketching an abstract pattern on a piece of paper. The room looks like a tiny home with a single bed, sofa, table with two plastic chairs, and a desk. The opposite wall opens into a bathroom no bigger than a closet, a heavy curtain the only offer of privacy.

Instead of windows, murals of nature scenes adorn white

concrete walls. And this mirror. This constant reminder of the fact that she has no privacy. No say in her own existence.

Prone to sudden aggression. I'm feeling prone to sudden aggression just seeing her there.

"Can I talk to her?" I clasp my hands together at my waist, hoping Marilyn won't see the tremble I can't seem to control.

"I was hoping you'd want to. I'm curious to observe what will happen. She has a Taser implant, so I can step in if she becomes agitated."

Marilyn unlocks the door, and I knock on the frame as I step inside. The door clicks shut behind me. The illusion of privacy, though I'm certain Vi isn't any more fooled than I am.

"Hi, Vi. My name's Hope. You don't have to speak, but I just wanted-"

"I know who you are."

I jump at the sound of her voice, raspy and halting. "Dr. Chambers is outside the window. You don't have to talk if you-"

She turns, her eyes boring into mine with an intensity that makes me take a step back.

"There can only be one Alpha. The two of us existing on this planet at once is unnatural. It's created a divide. I have the knowledge of our ancestors, while you have the love of our people. Neither of us can lead until those two halves are made whole."

My heart is racing. The shake in my hands is so bad, I cross my arms to contain it. I never imagined she would understand what we are... what we're meant to be. "How can we work together?"

"We can't."

"I don't understand. If we're two halves..."

"I couldn't bond, because I can't love. But Marilyn will figure it out. She's close. She knows it's in my blood. When it happens, it will tip the balance. I will have the strength of will to end your life, and then our people will love me as they've loved you."

I should be shocked at her words. I should argue and tell her there must be another way. But I know she's right. "Will that be best for our people?"

Vi laughs, and my skin crawls at the humorless tone and the sneer that could never pass as a smile.

"Stupid child." Vi stands, coming closer until her minty breath is on my cheek. "The Alpha is the backbone of Shifter culture. She has always led and connected our people. But this bond, the one that makes us slaves to the humans, is not natural. It is what turned us from a peaceful species into a weapon for sale to the highest bidder."

"I know a good man. If I bond with him, he wouldn't use us."

Vi laughs again, her hand reaching up to touch the ends of my hair. "You will never cement the bond in time. Marilyn will figure out how to force it long before you clue in."

"Then tell me. Please."

"I will not. You are the half with the compassion. I am the half with the knowledge. Knowledge always wins over emotion."

"Please. Tell me what to do."

"And give you the strength to end my life?"

"I would never-"

"You would. Because there is only one Alpha. This need for an artificial bond shackles us, but we are still Shifters."

"What if I died now?" Vi pulls back to look me in the eyes. Hers are wild with excitement, or something resembling it. I swallow past the lump in my throat. "Would that give you the strength to stop her from completing the Alpha bond?"

"Yes." Vi's response is immediate. The familiar tingle gathers at the back of my neck.

"And if I got you out of here, would you bond with someone good and protect our people? Would you keep the Meadow safe?"

"Yes. Yes, of course."

"Make me believe you."

"I give you my word."

"You're lying." I hate to accuse her, even though I know it's the truth. "I can feel it. The deception. You've told me only truth until I asked if you would keep the Meadow safe."

She growls low in her chest. I brace for her anger, but she simply returns to her desk and her drawing.

"*I know a good man.*" She laughs as she repeats my words, causing heat to rise in my cheeks. "You'll never bond before Marilyn."

Her tone more than her words sends an icy shiver across my skin. I need to bond with someone I can trust, and I need to do it before Marilyn finishes what she started. If she's right; if sex and love are somehow the magic combo... I need to find Gideon.

Despite what happened in the alley, and my doubts about his intentions, he's still the only human that even comes close to meeting that criteria.

How the heck am I going to start that conversation?

ORDERS

*F*uck, this is really it. I've been through the possible scenarios frontways and back, but no matter how I look at it, this needs to happen. The only way to protect the Meadow, and Hope, is to staunch the flow of newly awakened Shifters.

Cade met with the Elders to approve the plan and finalize the paperwork. If anyone questions our actions, I've got the official orders in my back pocket. This is what needs to happen.

Fuck, it's a hard pill to swallow.

He said he threw in a good word for me while he was there, insisting I didn't know what Hope was. I'm not convinced they bought it, especially if they spoke to the other men that were there that night. But I gotta give the guy credit for sticking his neck out. And I haven't been told to take a walk yet, so I guess that counts for something.

"Ready to go, man?" Cade's been eager to get this over with, but judging by the dark circles under his eyes, I'd bet he's been having just as much trouble dealing with what's coming as I have.

I open the driver's door and get out of my truck, hearing Cade's heavy boots on the pavement behind me.

BioSol Labs is an impressive place. At the edge of Moridian nearest Morwood Forest, it's a sprawling complex that manages to look both inviting and foreboding. I guess it depends on your reason for visiting. Today it looks pretty fucking dim despite the sun glinting off the white concrete and glass exterior.

When we enter the reception area, I don't bother taking a number.

"Hello, sir..." The receptionist's voice trails off when he looks up to see two Elites towering over his desk.

"Elite Gideon. I'm here for an order."

He seems to have a little trouble getting his eyes off us and back to his monitor, but when he does it only takes a few keystrokes to have him nodding. "It's ready for pickup." He gestures to the door at the left of his desk. "Just head through there and Dr. Chambers will meet you in room C."

"Thanks, man," Cade says.

It doesn't take long for the lead Scientist of the Shifter program to join us in the small consultation room. She's carrying what looks like an armored briefcase, trying unsuccessfully to hide how much she's struggling to lift the thing.

"Hello, Elites." She sets the case on a metal table. "Can I speak freely?"

"Of course, Doctor. And you should be aware that your surveillance systems will power down in our immediate vicinity for the duration of our stay."

"Understood." She nods, chewing on her lower lip before continuing. "Forgive me for being blunt, but this is an unusual request. The tranquilizer rounds in this case are each strong enough to take out an elephant. And there's two thousand of them."

"That's correct."

"The request stated they were for restocking the Protector's stockpile, but-"

"That's also correct. Thank you for your assistance, and your discretion." It's the story we're sticking with, even though it must be obvious to her there's enough tranq there to take out every active Shifter and then some.

She nods, but she's far from satisfied with our explanation.

"As head of the Shifter program here at BioSol, it's imperative that I be informed of any major changes forthcoming in the government's use of Shifter technology."

I pull the ordinance out of my back pocket and hand it to her. "This is all I'm permitted to divulge."

She reads the paper, then reads it again. A deep crevice forms between her eyes as her shoulders square.

"Why?"

"I'm sorry, Doctor. Those are my orders."

Her eyes narrow as she crosses her arms. "No. I won't allow it. I want to speak to the Elders directly. They don't understand what they're asking."

"You're welcome to request an audience. But this is starting now."

She looks back at the papers, her eyes darting over the words again as if looking for a loophole. She won't find any. It's black and white. All Shifters in BioSol Labs are to be euthanized.

"As you wish. Follow me to the nursery."

Cade picks up the briefcase, and we follow Dr. Chambers. Smart move, starting with the nursery. If anything can get us to back out of this whole shitshow, it'll be that room.

When we step into the brightly lit space, I'm instantly taken back. The day I came here to pick out my Shifter seems like a lifetime ago. Multiple lifetimes ago. I was young, cocky, and invincible in my own mind. I went straight for the biggest creature I could find; a grizzly.

I was clueless. The practicality of spending every waking moment with a bear is just ridiculous. He was big, loud, hairy and had the appetite of, well, a grizzly. It didn't take me long to wish I'd picked a bobcat.

Still, as much of a pain in the ass as he was, Tarek was loyal to a fault. I guess all Shifters are. When he took his dragon form for the first time, I couldn't have been prouder if I'd done it myself.

But then Damon came along and shattered that reality for both of us. If I was proud to have a dragon at my beck and call, I'm far prouder to consider Tarek a friend.

"Okay. Get your people in here and let's get this over with."

"Don't you want to do it yourself?"

"I'm just doing my job, Doctor. I don't take any pleasure in it. Your people can make this quick and humane."

"Right. Wait here, then."

"Elite Cade will accompany you. I'll be looking around on my own."

She opens her mouth to protest, but I make sure my expression lets her know it's pointless.

Cade will take the guided tour, drawing it out as long as he can. I'll poke around the places we aren't invited. We're hoping we learn something that changes the situation; new info or tech that gives us another option. I'm well aware it's unlikely.

She turns and heads for the back of the room, with Cade following on her heels. He looks back at me once, and for a moment my temper flares. I punch it down. I meant what I said to him at HQ. We've all done shit we're not proud of. Just because it's personal, doesn't mean I need to take it personally.

He's a valuable ally now. End of story.

I don't expect Dr. Chambers to show us all her cards, but

what she doesn't know is that I have a master key; a code that will open any lock I find. Precisely the tool I needed when I came here looking for Hope and couldn't get past the front door.

I also have full schematics of this place loaded and visible through my Comm implant, along with real-time infrared. All the tools needed to keep this nice and quiet. Thank you, Elders.

Time to do some recon.

One door at a time, room after room. For a research and development wing, there doesn't seem to be a lot of activity. I take a photo of each Shifter I find, noting their location.

A cougar in a metal kennel, dopey from sedation. A tiger in a holding room, pacing and panting and not the least bit interested in looking my way. Each one I come across is the same; so accustomed to being viewed and ignored, they don't care one way or the other about my presence. It's impossible for me to tell what their purpose is.

The next unmarked door leads to a corridor of more doors. Each one with a window beside it made of one-way glass. I can see in, but the poor soul inside can't see out.

I look in the first room, and inside is a tiny apartment.

Fuck. When I imagined the Shifters being kept here, I pictured them in animal form. I should have anticipated the lab would be aware of their ability to take human form.

I press my fingers into my temples, attempting to force my mind to readjust. Regardless of the form they're in, we need to euthanize all the Shifters we find. It's not just my orders, it's what needs to happen to prevent humans discovering the location of the Meadow.

How I feel about it is irrelevant.

I move to the next window, and the next. Relieved each time I find an empty room.

At the sixth window, the floor drops out from under me.

I grip the frame to steady myself as I look in at Hope. She's wearing loose, gray pants and a pale green shirt. She's stretched out on the bed, hands behind her head with her moonlit hair splayed out around her. Her eyes stare blankly up at the ceiling.

I key in my passcode and push the door open, expecting to find her sedated, confused, terrified.

She sits up, her eyes flying wide for just a moment before she launches herself at me. Her slender, strong arms wrap around my neck and I breathe in the fresh scent of her.

"Hope."

"Gideon!" She pulls back, looking up at me with clarity and surprise. "What are you doing here?" She rubs her hands over my chest and down my arms as if she can't believe I'm real.

"What are *you* doing here?" I turn the question back on her, restraining myself from patting her down for my own reality check. "You were supposed to be back at the Meadow. Tarek said-"

She slaps a hand over my mouth. "Shhh! They can see us!"

She points up at a camera in the corner, but I shake my head.

"It's blocked. We're alone. Tell me what's going on... how did they catch you again?"

She shakes her head. "It's not like that. I came back."

"You came back?"

"Yes." She pushes past me, looking out the door before closing it and pressing the lock. "I felt something. Someone. Oh, Gideon... how much time do we have alone?"

"I don't know. Enough for me to get you the fuck out of here."

"No. I can't. I..." She's looking at me with a desperate expression that makes me want to throw her over my shoulder and break down every door between here and freedom.

I can't help myself. I reach out and cup her face, running

my thumb along her bottom lip. I didn't expect to see her again. Not after the alley, and definitely not after the job I've got ahead of me.

"Hope, I need to tell you-"

"We need to have sex. Now."

My hand's still on her face as the blush colors her cheeks. I don't know what the punch line is, but my cock is hard as steel and ready to go the moment the words leave her lips.

"Hope..." I can hear the rough edge in my voice. Fuck. I want her desperately. If I could go back to those moments I had with her in my flat... How the fuck could I have let my past keep me from being with this woman when I had the chance?

I held everything in the palm of my hand, and I let it slip away.

I lean down, my heartbeat taking on an erratic rhythm as I brush my lips against hers. She leans into me, deepening the kiss with an urgency that makes my head spin.

"Gideon," she breathes my name on a sigh as she pulls away. "I'm not a natural-born Shifter. I was made here."

"What are you-"

"It's called the Alpha gene."

"So, if Dr. Chambers figures out how to force a bond with this other Alpha, she'll be in control of all Shifters."

I filled Gideon in on everything I've learned in as few words as possible. I don't know how much time we have alone, and I need him to see the urgency of my proposition. "And I won't survive it, or at least I'll lose my ability. There can only be one Alpha. When one of us bonds, it will tip this unnatural balance we seem to have."

"And that's why we need to-"

"Have sex. Yes. Now." I'm glad my words sound confident, because I can't muster enough courage to look him in the eyes. "It's not that I want to be Alpha... I don't. But I've met Vi and Marilyn. Neither one of them cares about protecting our people. The Alpha is supposed to be a connector, but they've twisted it and made us into weapons. If I bond with you, it stops them and gives us time to figure out the next step."

"If it works, will you be able to stop the newly awakened from leading people to the Meadow?"

"I'm not sure…"

"They're drawing too much attention. They need to be stopped, one way or another."

I don't like the way he says that last part. One way or another? Back in that alley, Cade said Gideon wanted to kill them all. I shudder at just the thought that Gideon might go so far.

"I wish I knew for sure, but I think so. I think I'll be able to reach them all."

"How do you know sex will trigger it? It seems a little... out there."

I look up at him, but his eyes are unfocused. No one in their right mind would want to do such a thing under these circumstances. Gideon has his own complications with sex, which only makes it worse that I'm putting him on the spot like this.

"I don't know for sure. I know sex doesn't do it, and neither does love. Maybe both together..."

His gaze snaps to me, and I can't look at him. Instead, I look down at the floor, at his boots. They're bulky enough to be considered weapons in their own right. In fact, he's wearing all his gear and weapons…

"Why are you here?" I ask again. He didn't answer me the first time, but what possible reason could he have for being in this part of the lab?

"I'm not good, Hope. I don't deserve your... I don't deserve you."

He's still avoiding my question. It doesn't matter. He's here, and his timing feels a lot like fate.

"Whether or not you deserve me has nothing to do with the way I feel. I'm not asking you for a commitment. Shifter females have very reliable fertility cycles, so you don't have to worry about being tied to me with young."

I hate how clinical this sounds, when the truth is the thought of being with Gideon makes my heart soar. But not here. Not like this, with me pressuring him into something he's not ready for.

"You think it's the best chance we have of stopping them and protecting the Meadow?"

"I think so. I know you don't-"

His hand on my cheek makes me stop mid-sentence, and when I hazard a glance, I'm surprised to see a playful smirk on his face.

"I've had far more unpleasant missions over the course of my career."

I cover my face with my hands, unable to help myself from laughing at the absurdity of this whole scenario. He takes my wrists and pulls them away from my face.

"I've regretted not being with you when I had the chance." His eyes hold mine, all trace of humor gone. "I'll only do this on one condition."

"What is it?" Blazes, I swear someone turned up the heat in here.

He leans down to brush his lips across mine, the delicate contact lighting a fire under my skin. "When all this is done, you give me the chance to do it right. To make love to you like you deserve. All night."

Oh, blazes. The shiver that runs through me at his words is

nearly orgasmic. All I can do is nod in agreement, as images of us wrapped in each other play through my mind.

He backs up a step, pulls out his comm, and types with quick thumbs. "We've got twenty minutes. Thirty tops before I'm expected back."

"Is that enough? It's a lot of pressure..."

In the space of a heartbeat, my back is pinned against him. One hand holds me tight, while the other runs a slow path down my belly. My body is putty in his arms as he trails kisses from my shoulder, up my neck.

"Just touching you makes me so fucking hard." His voice is a low rumble in my ear, as his hand slips past the waist of my BioSol inmate pants. "The thought of being with you is all the foreplay I need."

His fingers slide lower, finding that sweet spot that makes me arch my back and bite my lip to keep from crying out. He knows exactly how to touch me to make me delirious with need, teetering on the precipice after mere moments. He bites my neck, and I fly over the edge.

When I come back down, he scoops me off my feet and lays me on the bed. I'm still half dazed as he peels my pants off and crawls over me. His thick thighs push my legs wide, and I can't wait to feel him inside me. I don't care where we are, I don't care why we're doing this.

I run my hands up over his arms and down over his torso. He's still fully dressed, covered in weapons, and wearing those shit-kicker boots.

"Is this okay?" He asks with a voice as deep and rough as I've ever heard it. "I don't want to be unprepared if someone finds us."

I laugh as I reach between us to find the zipper on his pants. "Would you think I was weird if I said it's kind of sexy?"

He laughs with a low rumble, covering my mouth with a

hungry kiss that I eagerly return. It's way more than just kind of sexy. This man is deadly even when he's naked. Like this, he's lethal. Being pinned under all that strength and weaponry, completely at his mercy...

He swats my hand away as it becomes obvious I can't figure out how his pants work. A second later, as his tongue does wicked things with my mouth, the smooth, thick head of him presses against my core.

I can't help but moan as I lift my hips toward him, shamelessly begging for more.

"Are you sure about this, Hope?"

I can barely think straight, but he keeps just out of reach, waiting for my reply.

"I've wanted to be with you since you kissed me at the lake." I want to give him all the reassurance he needs. This might be the wrong setting, but it's definitely the right man. "Even if this doesn't work, I won't regret it. We'll do it right, just like you said."

He kisses me softly, then leans back just enough to look into my eyes as he pushes inside me. I watch his expression as his lips part and his breathing becomes unsteady. All the stress, worry, and grief that seemed to be a permanent part of him melts away until his face is a mask of pure pleasure.

I've never felt anything like this. He stretches me, fills me beyond anything I could have imagined. He's going slow, being careful, but I'm so ready for him I just want it all now.

I wrap my legs around his hips, urging him deeper as his weapons dig into my thighs. He gives me what I want, and even with his clothing between us, I feel him touching every part of me.

"Are you okay?" His words are unsteady. It's been so long for him. He's denied himself for years.

"You don't need to be gentle." I take his face in my hands, looking deep into his eyes. "Fuck me, Gideon."

My own words take me by surprise, but they release something carnal in him. His mouth crashes into mine as he takes me hard and fast. He braces himself up on his arms, adjusting the tilt of his hips until he finds that perfect angle. I grip the straps that curve around his shoulders, grinding my teeth to keep from screaming.

"Fuck, I love you." He growls the words, but I'm too lost in the sensations to respond.

My orgasm hits me so hard I lose all track of reality. There's nothing but pleasure as it consumes me in wave after wave of pure bliss.

When it recedes, Gideon's laying on his back and I'm wrapped in his arms with my head on his chest. His heart's racing and his breathing is as rough as mine.

"Are you okay?" I ask him, and he chokes out a laugh.

"I guess we didn't need twenty minutes."

I slap his stomach, but it's hardly effective considering my bones are made of jelly. I rub my thighs together just a little, feeling the evidence that he came right along with me.

He squeezes me a little tighter before letting me go to roll off the bed. "Don't move," he says as he heads into the tiny bathroom.

I close my eyes, content to bask in the afterglow for as long as I can. The bed dips, and a warm cloth presses against my thigh.

I watch his face as he washes me with gentle care. If there was any doubt in my mind that I've fallen for this man, it's long gone.

He said he loved me. I don't think it counts, considering the timing. Maybe he was just saying it to help secure the bond.

I don't care. I won't remind him or hold him to it, but I'll remember the sound of those words on his lips for the rest of my life.

When he finishes his gentle task, he returns to the bathroom to rinse the cloth. Reluctantly, I pull my discarded clothes back on and finger-comb my fine hair into a low pony.

Time to get back to reality. I sit on the edge of the bed and close my eyes, letting my mind go to that dark place full of all the sparks of Shifter consciousness. I'm not exactly sure what I'm looking for. Just any sign that the bond worked and I'm the Alpha.

Everything's the same. I don't feel any extra connection. I thought it would be... more.

I open my eyes. Gideon's standing in front of me, forehead creased and jaw clenched as if he's concentrating just as hard as I am.

"Did it work?"

"I don't know. I thought it would be obvious if it did... can you control me at all?"

I don't even know what that would feel like. Would it be like my body has a mind of its own? Or would it be less obvious, like an idea that seems to pop randomly into my head? Damon said it reminded him of his bond with Whisper, but I've never experienced that.

He shakes his head. "I've been trying to get you to kiss me, but you haven't gone for it."

I laugh, but the humor fades quickly.

It didn't work. I feel so stupid... I convinced him...

"I'll put her down." He states it with a casual tone, like he's talking about lunch instead of murder.

"What? No, I..."

My words trail off because as much as that idea goes against everything I stand for, I can't think of an alternative. It's her, or me. If I thought for one second that she would be a good Alpha, that she would do what's best for Shifters...

"I'll do it." Bile rises in the back of my throat.

"No." He drops to his knees in front of where I sit, grips my hands in his, and waits for me to meet his stare. "You're a healer. A connector. Goodness and light and I'm... I already have enough blood on my hands that a little more won't make any difference."

I look away as tears spill down my cheeks. I wanted this to work. I wanted love to be the answer.

"I'm sorry." His thumb brushes a tear from my cheek. "Is there another option?"

I close my eyes, trying desperately to come up with something. I already know there's nothing.

"I want to talk to her first. Alone."

He nods, helping me to my feet and pressing a kiss to my lips. Even in the midst of all this, my desire for him flares to life. It seems surreal that just minutes ago we were joined. I can still feel the pleasant burn that remains from the way he filled me so completely. I kiss him back, pulling his lower lip between my teeth and savoring the taste of him.

Neither one of us says another word as we slip out of the room and into the hallway. I know where to find her, in her prison cell disguised as a home.

ALPHA

I can see through the glass that she's awake, sitting at her desk just as she was the first time we met. Gideon types a code into the lock, and I knock softly before slipping inside.

"Hey, Vi."

She looks at me with narrowed eyes, and I'm certain she can tell why I'm here. I can't look at her. At those eyes that could be my own.

"What did you do?"

"I tried to bond. I tried the only thing I could think of that would work, but it didn't."

She laughs, and heat rises into my cheeks.

"Stupid child." She waves me away.

"Is there any way we can both live? Is there any way we can keep Marilyn, or someone like her from forcing a bond? Tell me now, Vi, because we're out of time."

She shakes her head, a smile spreading across her face that makes my stomach turn. "It's already too late. Marilyn almost has it. When it happens, I'll have all the power. She'll let me out of here, and I'll live like the Alpha I was meant to be."

"She'll sell her services to the highest bidder. You'll be used to control Shifters. To do whatever they want of you."

"I don't care. Let them destroy each other. I'll even control you, if you survive. And I'll take any mates I want." Her eyes light up as if the thought just occurred to her. "There're Shifters strong enough to take dragon form. Three of them. I'll have them all."

Her words leave me with no choice. My purpose is to protect Shifters, but I can't protect Vi. I can't keep her safe, or help her heal from this life of captivity, without risking every other Shifter's life. She's left me no choice.

I push off from the wall as I slip effortlessly into my wolf form.

Vi registers the attack too late, her eyes flying wide just before my jaw closes around her neck.

I don't hesitate. I bite and twist, feeling the pain and the panic as if my own life were ending. When I release her, her body crumbles to the floor and blood spreads in a growing pool around her ruined neck.

I turn away and vomit, heaving uncontrollably long after there's anything left in my stomach.

IT HAPPENS SO FAST, I don't have time to react until it's too late.

I'm watching through the one-way mirror as Hope talks with the other Alpha; a woman who looks like Hope might in thirty years. I can't hear what they're saying, but by the look on the older woman's face, she's enjoying the conversation a lot more than I'd expected her to.

In a blur, Hope's wolf dives forward. Her jaws close around the woman's neck, and I hear myself shout something even I don't understand as I pull my pistol and push through the door.

Inside the room, I holster my weapon. Hope's turned away from the body, the white fur on her face and chest stained crimson. She's vomiting violently, and I curse out loud at my stupidity for letting her come in here first.

She doesn't deserve this. The guilt will haunt her for the rest of her life.

I pull out my comm, letting Cade know that I'm bailing and he needs to abort immediately. Orders be damned. I don't wait for a response.

"We need to get out of here, now. You need to get back to the Meadow."

She looks up at me, and her eyes are so dark they're more black than violet. I need to get her to safety.

She seems to snap out of her haze as she lurches forward, pushing past me to run into the hall. I lead us through the shortest route possible, avoiding BioSol employees until we push through a side exit into the open air.

I haul ass to my truck, and Hope leaps through the driver's door onto the passenger seat. A second later, we're laying down rubber. She could have just made a run for the forest straight from BioSol, but the risk of being tracked is too great. Better to put some distance behind us first.

I don't know how I'll explain my actions back there, but that's a problem for later. Keeping her safe is all that matters.

I glance at her as we drive. She's sitting in human form, and there's no trace of the blood and gore that marred her wolf's fur.

"We're not being followed," I assure her, even though I'm watching my rear-view as intently as the road ahead.

She looks at me, and I'm relieved to see the soft, violet iris's back to their normal shade. Please don't let this kill her spirit.

If I had just gone in there first. I can take down a mark and sleep like a baby. Killing people that don't deserve to live is as easy as breathing. Hope's not wired that way. She's not a killer.

She nods, turning to look out the window as we cruise past buildings and vehicles. I throw it in park at the edge of the city, then run while Hope lopes beside me in wolf form. When we finally reach the shelter of Morwood, I sink down onto my ass to catch my breath.

Hope shifts and bursts into tears.

"Goddamnit," I curse as I pull her against me. She fits just perfectly between my thighs and against my chest as I wrap my arms tight around her.

"I'm sorry," she says as she buries her face in my chest, her small body wracked with silent sobbing.

"Easy. You were so brave. You did the right thing. You were so fucking brave." I keep repeating the words in low tones, and little by little she seems to relax.

When her breathing is steady again, she lifts up to look at me. Her expression is one I haven't seen before.

"I felt it. When I... When she... I felt it like it was my neck. My life. I felt her dying."

Fresh tears spring from her already bloodshot eyes, but she takes a deep breath and wipes them away.

"I'm so sorry."

"It had to be me. She deserved nothing less."

I nod as my chest swells with pride for this incredible woman. She didn't react out of impulse or anger, or even to spare me from the unpleasant task as I'd feared. She gave her opponent an honorable death.

"Marilyn almost has it figured out. I can feel it now, like Vi could. Her blood is my blood."

"Can Dr. Chambers force the bond with you now? Even from a distance?"

"I think so, yes. I need to bond before she finishes."

"I'm all for trying again..."

She punches my shoulder, my attempt at humor bringing a brief smile to her face. Fuck, I wish I could fix this for her, so that smile could stay. So we could stay.

She pushes up to her feet and brushes dead leaves off her pants. "No. I had it all wrong. I need to get back to the Meadow."

"Go." I pull her close, kissing her mouth and then resting my forehead on hers. "And be safe."

No sooner are the words out of my mouth, when the trees shudder and a dragon's roar splits the air.

"I already called our ride." She flashes me a wide smile, and I must look like a deer in headlights as I gape at her.

She did it. She's their Alpha.

"Wait." I grab her arm as she starts toward the edge of the trees. "Can you do it now? Can you communicate with them all?"

"Yeah, I guess I can."

I pull her back to me and kiss her with a bruising intensity that barely expresses the force of my emotion.

We push through the brush to find Tarek and Damon, saddled and ready. They both have their eyes locked on Hope, and I recognize the look in Tarek's. He's talking to her, they both are, just like Tarek and I can do with our Link.

I look at Hope. I can't believe I had her in my arms, if only for a moment.

"Let's go." She says, flashing me a smile before she jogs over to Damon.

SACRIFICE

"There's no time to explain what I'm about to ask."

Whisper nods, her eyes holding mine with firm confidence. She ran to meet us the moment we touched down at the edge of the Meadow.

Her eyes dart to Damon over my shoulder, then back to me. "Damon said you called to him."

I want to tell her everything, but I can sense the urgency in my veins. Marilyn is far too close.

"If your death, here and now, would stop Shifters from being controlled... would you lay down your life?"

I hear Damon's growl of protest from behind me, but he won't interfere. No matter what I do, he won't challenge me.

"Yes, of course. Are you..."

Her voice trails off, her brow knitted in concentration. She presses a hand against her stomach, and I know I'm asking for far more than her life alone.

"I'm their Alpha. Your blood, will you give it to set us free?"

"Yes."

Her response is immediate and sure. She may not be a

Shifter, but somehow I've earned the trust and loyalty of this fierce woman.

"Give me your knife."

Damon's agony slices through my heart as his knees hit the ground. Whisper pulls a thick blade from a sheath on her thigh and hands it to me without hesitation.

"Your wrist."

She holds her hand toward me, eyes wide and jaw set. As fearful as she is determined. I slide the sharp blade over both our palms, then grip her hand in mine. As our blood mingles, I watch the realization dawn in her eyes.

"We are bonded. As long as you live, no one else will ever control us."

Her eyes fill with tears as I release her hand, and she holds her bloody palm to her chest. The moment I drop my hold on him, Damon crashes into her, holding her tight and whispering pure love into her ear.

It's in my blood. Those were Vi's words, but I didn't understand how literal she meant it. The simple connection of blood and unwavering trust. Marilyn had the blood, but she never had Vi's trust, which is why she had to find an artificial way to force it. And Gideon... I love him. I do. But I can't say I trust him completely. Not like I trust Whisper.

"I'm sorry I had to do that. I had to be sure you would put Shifter's first, at all costs. We're safe now."

Whisper closes her eyes as she leans into Damon. "I'm honored, Hope."

A cool hand on my arm makes me jump, and I look to see that our display has drawn a growing crowd. Father's nowhere to be seen, but I rest a hand on my mother's for a moment before pulling her into a hug.

She stiffens at the unexpected gesture. When she relaxes, I

speak for only her to hear. "I understand now, why you acted the way that you did."

When I pull away, her eyes are brimming with tears.

"You may not be mine, but I carried you and I gave birth to you. I loved you the moment I held you in my arms."

"You were afraid." I feel the emotion in her even now.

"Yes." She lowers her eyes. "I tried to keep my distance, because I could lose you at any moment. If you learned the truth, or if you bonded... I..."

"I understand." It's the best I can offer her. It's the truth. She nods, swiping tears from her cheeks as she turns to hurry away. She never liked showing emotion in front of others.

I look back toward Gideon. He's talking with Tarek, Whisper, and Damon. He glances my way and gives me a wink that makes my skin warm.

The entire Meadow is gathered now. I close my eyes, accessing the memories and wisdom of my predecessors that were locked away like a secret library in my mind. It's a heady feeling, and I could so easily get lost in it.

"I am our Alpha." I talk to them not only with spoken words, but also through the connection we now share. "I connect us to each other, and to our history. Our ancestors were taken from their planet. They were experimented on and modified until they became tools to be sold and bought and used. Knowing who we are, and where we come from, is the first step in gaining our freedom."

When I stop talking, the crowd buzzes with excitement and conversation. I'm bombarded with attention as the people I've known my entire life suddenly want to touch me and tell me how they've always felt a connection with me. It's odd, but it also feels right.

When Luke stands in front of me, looking a little smaller

than usual, there's only one thing I want to say to him. "Thank you, Luke."

He looks at me like I've grown a second head, but he takes my hand when I offer to shake. "You were loyal to my parents, even when you didn't agree with what they asked of you. You watched my back and helped keep the Meadow safe, even if you were kind of a dick about it."

He chokes on a laugh, and just like that, the tension between us is gone. His face grows serious again as he grips my hand a little tighter. "I'm loyal to you now, Hope. Whatever you need."

"Thank you."

At last, I've greeted everyone in turn. Even my snarky brothers were compelled to touch my hands and offer words of support. With the crowd dispersed, I take a moment in silence, closing my eyes to rest in the Darkness that felt so sinister for so long. Now, it's home. It's where I can let go of me, and be We.

Refreshed, I walk to where Gideon, Tarek, Damon and Whisper still stand together. One look at Gideon and I know he wants to kiss me as badly as I want to kiss him. I don't need a bond to feel that kind of connection. But he stands still, arms crossed, looking like the deadly Protector he is.

Tarek's grinning like a kid, as his eyes dart from Gideon to me and back again. Damon just looks tired, and I'm hit with a fresh stab of guilt for what I put him through. He nods, offering me a weak smile. He understands, and that's enough for now.

"Whisper, can I talk to you alone?"

"Of course." She gives Damon a soft, lingering kiss, then follows me into the privacy of the trees.

"This isn't the end."

"I know."

"We stopped the most urgent threat, but I could still be used to hurt my people if someone gets to you."

"I know. And I'll be careful. Not that I couldn't defend myself, but Damon won't be letting me out of his sight any time soon. And Tarek insists he'll be roasting anyone who looks even remotely suspicious. Not to mention the rest of the fighters in this place, who are improving by the day, thanks to yours truly. And Gideon..." She looks at me with a knowing spark in her eyes, and I'm sure the color in my cheeks confirms her suspicions.

"He's a good man," I say. And I mean it. Whatever he was involved in, I know in my heart he was doing what he thought best for the Meadow.

"He is. He deserves to be happy."

I nod, but her words have me swiping tears off my cheeks.

"I can feel the unawakened Shifter's, but I can't reach them. There's some that are newly awakened, but I can't seem to talk to them, either."

"We will. When the Meadow is fortified, we'll find them. They'll all have the chance to be free."

"I can connect us, give us a history, a future, and lead us as we figure out how to coexist with humans. That's the way it should be. But as long as I'm here, evil people will do evil things to get to me."

"We won't let that happen."

"And when they find out who I've bonded with, they'll want you, too. They'll use the ones you love against you."

"I would never betray you, or the Meadow."

"If they got to Damon? If they got to your child?"

Whisper's eyes cloud with grief. "I didn't... we don't know for sure if I'm..."

"No one would blame you for sacrificing everything to protect your family. It's a choice I never want you, or anyone, to have to make. I can only imagine the love you must feel... I can only wish..."

"If the way Gideon's been looking at you is any indication, I'd bet your going to get that wish."

That thought almost makes me smile. "Don't. We both know I can't stay."

"What are you saying, Hope?"

"On our natural planet, the Alpha connection was an evolutionary advantage that kept us safe against predators that make dragons look like geckos. But here, with humans as our enemy, our strength has become our weakness. This artificial bond makes us vulnerable. They won't stop trying to use it against us."

"So, we hide here and we fight. We make damn sure neither one of us ends up anywhere near those people."

"I can't live, Whisper. Tell me I'm wrong? Tell me you wouldn't come to the same conclusion if our roles were reversed?"

She opens her mouth to argue, but then bites her lip. She looks away.

"You held out your hand to me. You were willing to give your life, maybe even the life of your unborn child, to protect us against a threat you didn't fully understand. Don't tell me my people deserve anything less from me."

We stand in silence. There's nothing left to say. After a few minutes, I lead the way back to the clearing.

My heart does a little dance when Gideon is the first person I see. I want to melt into his arms. I want to kiss him in front of everyone. I just don't know if he would want that. Despite everything we've shared, I'm a different person than I was even a few hours ago.

"Can you communicate with them? All of them?"

It takes me a moment to understand what he's asking. "No... I can feel them, but I can't seem to reach them."

"I need to go back."

I'm speechless for a moment. Even though I questioned if he would still want me, I didn't expect him to be so certain. He turns away, but I grab his arm.

"You can't. They might have seen you leave with me. It won't be safe..."

"This isn't over yet, Hope."

His brow creases, but he looks me in the eyes with such intensity, I'm certain I don't want to hear what he's about to say.

"Before I found you at BioSol, my orders were to kill every Shifter. The young in the lab. The Protectors on duty. All of them. Those orders still stand, whether I'm there to carry them out, or not."

I let my hand drop from his arm. "I knew you were involved with something bad."

"If you can't call them back immediately, the threat still stands."

"Please tell me you can stop it now?"

"I'll do what I can." His pale eyes are icy, and I feel the chill down to my bones. "You need to get them to wake up and get out of the cities. The Meadow's still in danger. Maybe more so now that their weapon's been stolen. I'll do everything in my power to make sure no one finds this place."

He reaches out and runs his thumb across my cheek, and I lean into his touch. No matter what he's done, I can't change the way I feel about him. I wouldn't want to.

He turns and goes to Tarek, who's waiting in dragon form.

"You should say goodbye." Whisper grasps my hand. "He's lost so much, and if you... if you leave without saying good-bye." Her voice cracks, and I squeeze her hand.

"Don't worry. He's not going far."

She looks at me with raised eyebrows, and I can't stop my grin. There's no way I'm letting that man go without a proper, private, goodbye. I can only imagine how angry he'll be when he's told to sit and stay by a very persuasive Tarek.

But first, "I need to talk to my father."

"WHERE IS HE?"

Mother tips her head to the back room of their tent as she rolls her eyes. "He's packing his things."

She's trying very hard not to smile.

I push through the heavy flaps that separate the main room from their sleeping quarters, finding him fuming as he stuffs clothing into a canvas bag. I watch him in silence until he notices me.

"I'm your father. I raised you as my own. I'm your father in every way that matters."

"Did you ever love me? For one single moment, did you care about anything other than your experiment and the potential payday?"

He fumbles over some unintelligible words, but I don't honestly care one way or the other about his response.

"Build yourself a cabin. You can't leave, I'm sure that much is obvious." I turn to go, but I can't help but think however selfish his motives were, the Meadow might never have begun without him. "Besides, the kids would be disappointed if you weren't here to make them new toys."

I hear him suck in a breath, but I don't look back at his face.

On my way out, Mother blocks my path. "Hope, I want you to know that your father and I do love each other. It's been complicated from the beginning, and I haven't always agreed with him. But I do love him."

"He was packing to leave."

"He was."

"Were you going with him?"

She takes a deep breath. "I've been an Alpha here since we started this. Maybe not in the same way you are now, but I always did my best. I was confident you wouldn't be sending him away. In fact, I owe him a very satisfying 'I told you so' right about now." She smiles as she smooths the front of her shirt.

I feel some of the weight lift from my shoulders. When I'm gone, Mother will still be here. She was a good leader. She'll be an even better one without the constant threat of the secret she was keeping.

SAY YES

I slide to the ground and thank Damon for the lift. He takes off with a rumble in his chest, and the solitude of the lake wraps me in its comforting embrace.

But I didn't come here to be alone this time. Strong arms slide around my waist, pulling me back against the familiar wall of Gideon's chest.

"Tarek had a few interesting guesses about why you wanted him to leave me here."

"Did he now?"

I lean back into his strength, soaking up the heat of his body at my back as the still evening surrounds us. The air is heavy with the scent of forest, lake, and Gideon. Wispy clouds drift across the deep blue sky, as pink tints the spaces between the mountains.

My memory returns to what seems like a lifetime ago, when I first saw him here in the moonlight. He hugs me tighter as he presses a kiss to my shoulder, then my hair. The heat of his mouth caresses my neck and the course stubble on his face tickles my skin, causing a delicious sensation to ripple through me.

"I seem to recall we made a deal." My voice is breathy, my newfound Alpha confidence evading me.

I turn in his arms. The emotion in his eyes takes my breath away. I slide my hands up his stomach along the thick, rough material of his combat gear. My body ignites as I recall him braced over me, giving me his body. His heart.

"Can we steal this moment? Can we forget about everything, and just be happy for now?"

He presses his forehead to mine, our breath mingling in the space between us. "Are you sure that's okay?"

I brush my lips against his. It's not okay, but if it's all we get, I'll take it. I wrap my fingers around the harness that's strapped to his chest.

"I'd like to undress you, but I'm not sure I know how."

His smile consumes him, and then his hands are on my head and he's kissing me so fiercely I'm seeing stars. When he pulls back, he takes only a few seconds to shed his weapons. A hidden zipper runs from his neck, down his side, and he peels the heavy armor from his body.

With one hand he reaches over his head and grasps his undershirt, pulling it off in a tantalizing reenactment of the moment that fueled so many daydreams. This time, I'm not ashamed to be watching. This time, I can touch him. Taste him.

Anticipation has me nearly vibrating, but I'm also desperate to savor these moments. He stands still as my fingers map the veins that run along his arms, as I trace the contours of his chest, and the ridges of his abdomen. I press a kiss over his heart and taste his salty skin with the tip of my tongue.

He tugs at the hem of my shirt, and I raise my arms so he can pull it over my head. With deliberate care, he undresses us both until there's nothing left between us.

His kisses linger across my skin as he touches me like he

wants to memorize every curve and line. Everything he does makes me feel love so great I think my heart might burst.

The soft moss of the lakeside cradles me as his mouth burns a trail down my body. I arch into him as his kiss presses against my sex. I moan with unrestrained pleasure as his tongue delves deep and his hands work wicked magic on my breasts.

"Gideon." I breathe his name on a sigh, and he focuses on that sensitive nub as his tongue flicks like a hummingbird's wings. His name turns into a scream of pleasure as my entire body ignites.

He coaxes me through wave after wave of pure bliss, as I grab fistfuls of his hair and buck against him. I lose all track of reality, lost to the sensations and emotions.

Then he's hovering over me, watching my face with rapt attention as his hips settle between my thighs. When my eyes focus on his, he kisses me softly as the hard length of his arousal presses into my belly.

I'm desperate to feel more of him. I thread my fingers through his hair, pulling him down into a deeper kiss as I wrap my legs around his hips.

He takes the cue, pulling back before sinking into me with a moan of pleasure that echoes my own. He trembles as he kisses me, and I mold my lips to his; nipping and caressing as he moves inside me with slow, deliberate strokes.

It's intoxicating. I'm drunk on the feel of our bodies joined and our hearts beating as one. The sweetness of his pace, his kisses, it's almost too much for my heart to bear. I touch him everywhere I can reach, my fingertips mapping his body. Committing all of him and these moments to precious memory.

Another climax nears, and the gentle pace isn't enough. I growl, sounding more wolf than woman, as I dig my nails into his back and nip that dark trail of tattoos. He abandons restraint, his hips colliding with mine in a relentless tempo as I dig my fingers into his back to keep myself grounded.

Just when I think this man's shown me the limits of pleasure, he takes me to another level once again. Our bodies, our voices, and our pleasure are one as we fly apart together. I cling to him, and he holds me tight. Nothing matters beyond this moment that stretches into forever and ends far too soon.

As we come down, chests heaving, hearts pounding, and foreheads pressed together, I'm sure I've found the very definition of happiness.

He falls onto his back, pulling me with him to rest against his chest. Neither one of us speaks. Maybe he's just as lost in this moment as I am. Maybe he's just as reluctant to watch it end.

"I love you, Gideon." He sucks in a breath. "There's no future for us. I know that. But I wanted you to know how much you mean to me."

I didn't come here to corner him into confessing. Besides, he might not realize it, but I already have the memory of those words on his lips tucked away in my heart.

His arms tighten around me for a moment, and he moves until we're on our sides, facing each other. His hand runs a lazy path from my shoulder to my hip and back again.

"I wish we could give this... us, a real try. But you deserve someone with no reservations... no baggage."

"I don't want anyone else. There is only you, Gideon. There will only ever be you."

"I have to go-"

"I'd be a hypocrite if I asked you to stay. Don't come back for me. I won't be here even if you do."

Just like that, our moment's shattered. I want to take back my words, rewind time, and just stay lost in his eyes a little longer. But his face twists in confusion as he pushes up to his elbow, looking down at me.

"What do you mean? You can't leave now."

"I'm a weapon that's meant to be used against my own kind."

"No. You bonded with Whisper. No one can use you now."

I push up to my knees, taking his hand in both of mine to hold it against my heart. "As long as I live, they will try to control me. They will come for me, for Whisper, for the people we love. We stopped the threat today, but until I'm gone, they won't stop trying to use me."

"No." His tone is final, his eyes searching for something to focus on. "We'll find another way."

"I'm sorry, I-"

He grips my face in his hands, gently but firmly, forcing me to look him in the eyes. "No. Stay, please. I need you to stay."

"Don't do this. You have to see it's the only way. I can't let myself be used to hurt them."

"I won't let anyone near you."

I push away from him, standing up to put some distance between us. The brilliance of the sunset has passed, and the silver moon hangs above the mountain peaks. Goosebumps spread across my bare skin from the cool night air.

"You aren't staying anyway, Gideon. I shouldn't have said anything."

He spins me around to face him, his hands instantly warming me. His eyes are dark, his expression something desperate. "No. None of it matters if you aren't safe. Please. I can't lose you. I have to know you'll be safe."

"I love you, Gideon. But-"

"Stop saying that. I can keep you and the Meadow safe from out there. But you deserve a real mate. A Shifter mate."

"I waited for love, and I found you." I hate the pain that

flashes in his eyes, but I know my words are true. I can't say when it happened, but the more this beautiful man let me in, the farther I fell. But I also meant what I said; I won't be selfish. "But I need to put my people first. Nothing will change that."

"I can't lose you." His eyes are the greenest I've ever seen them, his voice a plea. "If you destroy yourself, you destroy me. I've lost people I've loved, but I've never loved like this."

My heart stops beating. I don't understand him. Why is he saying all this now? Just to convince me to stay alive, while he'll be miles away...

He pulls me tight against him, and even with the seriousness of the moment, his body naked against mine lights me on fire. It's the same for him, as I feel him growing hard between us. He presses a kiss to my mouth, then rests his forehead against mine.

"I love you. Don't go." His words are a plea, and they tear at my heart. "Stay, and I'll stay, too. Give me a chance to love you. I don't know if I'll be any good at it... but give me a chance."

I can't stop the tears that slide down my cheeks. His words are more than I could ever have imagined. "I want that more than anything, but my people have to come first."

THIS WOMAN. She gives herself to me even as she takes everything away. If I hadn't been so stupid. If I hadn't resisted loving her, being with her, maybe she wouldn't be so quick to jump to this insane conclusion.

There has to be another way. I pull her tighter against me, desperate to keep her body close as my mind races to find a solution that will solve everything.

There has to be a way.

"Your absence will only delay the inevitable. The Elder's will find this place and they'll want it destroyed. Lives will be lost even without you here. Especially without you here, because Shifters won't have the advantage of your connection."

"We're already preparing for an attack."

"What if we can prevent it..." I'm grasping at straws, but there's something there...

"How?"

"We fight them now, on their turf. We go public, tell everyone."

"Tell them what, exactly?"

"About all of you. Everything. We tell them about you, that you're their Alpha. Leader of all the Shifter's. I'm already a public figure. A fucking celebrity. I've never cared about all that, but it gives me visibility... people will listen."

"I don't see how that will do anything. All they will see is a Shifter breaking the law, and an Elite with a new pet."

Then it hits me, clear as day. It's so perfect, I can't believe it took this long.

I love this woman. She loves me.

For so long Lily, the baby, my mistakes... they seemed like too much to bear. I was so sure I'd never move on, so sure I didn't deserve to even try. But somehow being with Hope is just... right. She doesn't change what happened or take away my role in it. I see now that I can keep my grief and my guilt, but still live my life and learn to do better. I can love and be loved.

"What if you're my wife?"

"Excuse me?" She pushes out of my arms, and I reluctantly let her go. "You can't be serious?"

"I want you by my side, Hope. I want you safe, and in my arms. In my bed. I would have proposed to you the moment you arrived here at the lake if I'd thought for a second that staying with you would be the best thing for you."

"You can't marry someone just because it's a political advantage."

"Why not? You were planning to mate Tarek, just because your parents needed the leverage."

"That's not fair."

"No, it wasn't fair. But you were willing, regardless. I love you. I want to spend the rest of my life earning your trust and your love in return."

"You already have it."

"Then why does it matter if we rush this part a little?"

She tries to argue, but she can't come up with anything. I cross my arms, feeling a smug smile that I couldn't hold back if I tried. My smile only widens when she can't stop herself from checking me out.

I drink in the sight of her standing there, hands on her hips, naked, radiant in the afterglow of our lovemaking. I might have been perfectly fine avoiding sex for years, but now that I've been with Hope, I don't think I'll ever get enough.

I let her squirm for a little while before closing the distance between us and scooping her into my arms. She squeals as I head for the lake, plowing into the clear water to the beautiful sound of her laughter.

We make love until we're exhausted, then curl up together on the mossy shore. When we're woken by the chill, we begin again. In the lake, on the shore, against the smooth bark of a tree... we make love so many times I lose count as the moon travels too fast across the starry sky.

When my eyes open to the golden light of dawn, I'm not sure if my body is capable of moving. Hope stirs in my arms, and I swear if she starts touching me again, I'm going to have to tap into my Stim to keep up with her.

Thankfully, she seems content to stretch and yawn, running her fingers in lazy circles over my stomach as I do the same to her back.

"Marry me, Hope. Be my mate, and my wife."

"Gideon..." She sits up, looking down at me with the glow of the morning sun like a halo around her head.

I sit up, taking her face in my hands and making sure she sees how serious I am. "Say yes. To life. To me. To life with me."

She stares at me as those violet eyes blaze with emotion. Just when I think she might continue to refuse, she throws her arms around my neck.

"Yes, Gideon. Oh, please, yes."

Time stands still as everything clicks into place. Every moment, every decision I've ever made led me here, to Hope.

I'm lost in the perfection of it all.

So lost, I don't realize we're not alone until the black wolf is less than fifteen paces away.

I spring to my feet, tugging Hope up and behind me as I brace for an attack. The wolf stands between me and my discarded gear. I curse at my carelessness, as my naked, weaponless body doesn't leave me with much defense against such a creature.

A small, cloth bag drops to the sand as its lips peel back in a growl. I meet its eyes, and my stomach drops at the familiar violet hue.

"Vi?" Hope tries to step around me, but I keep her shielded with my arm. "I thought..."

Goddamnit. How could I not have made sure the job was done?

The wolf's body shudders, melting into the form of the woman I saw through the glass at the lab.

"You couldn't kill me. You're far too weak and sentimental."

"What are you doing here?" Hope tries to step closer to her, but I pull her back against me. I need my gear. There's not even a fucking stick within easy reach, and my body's hardly at full strength after last night.

I keep still, avoiding eye contact. The best I can hope is not to provoke her, though I doubt she came all this way just to chat. I use every tool at my disposal, silently running through scenarios as I calculate distances and trajectories to aid my reaction time for each possible outcome.

"Marilyn sealed the bond," Vi says.

"No. That's not possible, I..."

"I didn't think so either. Two Alphas shouldn't be possible. It's never happened. But here you are, and here I am."

Hope's breathing is fast and shallow. She grips my arm that's still blocking her. "What does it mean?"

"I see it now. I see all of them. They don't know me, but I know each of them just as you do. And now I know what you meant. Protecting our people is all that matters."

I feel Hope's immediate relief as her body relaxes, but I'm not so quick to trust. Hope wants to see the good. She wants a happy ending. But I know endings are often anything but.

"Vi, that's... amazing. I'm so-"

"But it doesn't matter how I feel. The humans have their weapon." Vi shakes her head, and I pull Hope tighter against me. "I'm here to kill you. Please, kill me first."

Hope's gasp of surprise turns to a scream as Vi leaps into her wolf form. I shove her with all my strength as I meet the beast head on.

The certainty of the fact that I won't survive this leaves me with nothing to hold back. The wolf's jaws are wide as it lunges for my face, and I throw a Stim-fueled punch right past those deadly fangs to the back of its throat.

She recoils, gagging, and I roll for my weapons. The wolf plows into me just as my hand closes around the hilt of my knife, pinning me back against the sand. Fuck, she's heavy. Jaws close around my neck, but her bite is weak from the hit she took.

My left arm is useless and I can't feel a damn thing, but there's a sickening pulling sensation in my gut that tells me the fucking clock is ticking.

I manage to get the knife out of its sheath and put everything I've got left into burying it in that fucker's hide.

My ears are ringing with the sound of Vi's feral growling, Gideon's furious roars, and screams that seem to be ripping from my chest of their own accord.

I scramble to get my footing after Gideon's shove leaves me sprawling on the sand, but in the second I take to shift, Vi's wolf is already on top of him. She clamps her jaws around his neck as her claws tear at his belly.

I can't pull her off, or her teeth will shred his neck. Instead, I snap and growl at her face, trying to get her to turn her attention to me. She doesn't budge.

I catch the glint of steel and scramble backward as Gideon sinks a knife into her side. He hits her again and again, until she finally collapses.

I jump in to pull her heavy body off him, and then I'm frozen.

No.

The howl that's ripped from my chest is a sound I've never

heard before, and as I shift back to human form it becomes a desperate, pleading cry.

I don't even know where to start. I grab my clothes, using them to staunch the blood from the deepest wounds on his abdomen, but it's too much. His neck, his arm, his chest and belly... please, oh please let him be unconscious.

I lean on him, using my body to press against the wounds I can't cover with my hands. I stare at his face. His beautiful face.

His eyelids flutter and open.

"No. Close your eyes. Rest. She's gone." God, please, don't let him feel this.

"Hope."

"Shhh. It's okay, just rest."

"Go to the Meadow. They know where we are."

"No. Tarek and Damon are on their way. We'll go back together."

He closes his eyes. Leaning my forehead against him, I give in to sobs that wrack my body. I cry and beg for his life until hands grip my shoulders. I fight against them, but Damon's familiar arms surround me as his voice murmurs against my ear.

"Take him," I say through my tears. "I don't have the equipment for the care he needs. Take him to a hospital."

My stomach churns as I watch Gideon's lifeless body lifted in Tarek's massive talons.

"What happened here?"

I look up at Damon. My legs must have given out, because I'm sitting in a heap on the sand. He's shirtless, and I look down to see I'm wearing an oversized black t-shirt. Gideon's drying blood coats my skin.

I tell Damon everything that happened when Vi arrived. Everything she said.

"She wanted me to kill her. She wanted to protect our people..."

"Fine fucking way of showing it."

"Damon..."

"Come on, let's get you back. I'll scout to see if there's any more trouble coming once you're safe in the Meadow."

He moves around, gathering Gideons clothes and weapons. When he picks up the cloth bag Vi brought, I scramble to snatch it from his hands.

I don't know what I'm expecting to find, but I turn my back to him as I open the clasp and peer inside. I close it just as quickly.

Why would she bring this here?

HONOR'S MINE

*T*ake me home.

Thank fuck for our Link, because I couldn't speak if I tried. And I'm fairly certain I'm flying in Tarek's dragon hands, but with the way reality is fading in and out, I could be anywhere.

Shit, brother. You are seriously fucked up. I'm taking you to a hospital.

Home.

No way, G. You—

Home. They die.

It's the best argument I can manage before I black out again.

When I force my eyes open, I'm flat out on my living room floor covered in a heavy blanket. The smell of blood, sweat and coffee confirms I'm not dead just yet. My Medic implant is clearly working overtime.

They know where the Meadow is.

"Get me a Medic shot." Fuck, my voice sounds as butchered as I feel.

"I hit you already. Morphine too. Tell me why the fuck I brought you here instead of a hospital?"

Tarek's sitting on the sofa, elbows braced on his knees. Hell, if he hit me with a shot on top of my implant, it must be grim.

"You really think it would have made a difference?"

"Hell, G. I don't know. I'm no fucking doctor."

"They know where the Meadow is."

His eyes go wide, and I hope he knows how much that fact changes everything. "Fuck. You sure?"

"Yeah."

The moment Vi bonded, the moment she connected, it was done. Her own words confirmed it; *I see all of them.* If she knew, BioSol knows. It's only a matter of time before the intel reaches the Elders, if it's not there already.

"Brother, let me take you to a hospital."

"No time. Could be a Destroyer over already."

"Fuck." He stands up, fists balled at his sides. "You think that's how it will go?"

"Wall was never going to stop it. Be a crater before they risk the political fallout of it becoming public." I can't take a full breath. Hell, is that sound coming from my lungs? "Hit me again. Two more."

"What the fuck? You want to go dancing one last time before you check out?"

"Fuck yeah."

He's silent, but he walks to the bathroom and back.

"This is gonna juice you like a fucking superhero."

"I'm counting on it."

"You know what's gonna happen when you crash."

"Like a bug on a windshield. Only need a couple hours."

He's quiet. Thinking. I need him to hurry the fuck up. I might feel half decent after the morphine he gave me, but the darkness around the edges of my vision isn't very promising.

"Why do you care this much?"

"I'm dead, anyway. Might as well make it count for something."

"No. You were risking yourself for Shifters, for me, before this."

I take a minute to get my thoughts just right. Not an easy task at the moment. "I'm a Protector. I guess I found something that deserves to be protected."

He hits me with a shot in each thigh, and I swear my nervous system lights up like a Christmas tree. I close my eyes, giving in to a moment of remembering what it felt like to hold Hope, to think that loving her, marrying her, might solve all of this.

Then I'm off the floor, stumbling around like I'm driving a fucking mech for the first time instead of trying to control my own limbs.

I make it to the bathroom, confirming in the mirror that my wounds are sealing. Fuck, I'm a mess. I turn on the water and scrub off as best I can manage.

A little steadier on my legs, I go to the bedroom and retrieve a spare comm from the safe, then contact the Elders to arrange an emergency debriefing. I pull on tactical gear and load every weapon I can fit on my body.

I've got hours at best, before the toll this is taking on my organs shuts me down for good. Maybe I'll get lucky and last in a coma long enough to be officially declared a traitor.

"Drop me off at HQ, then get the fuck out of town."

Tarek grabs my head and presses his forehead against mine. "It's been an honor, Gideon. I'll make sure they know you went out like a fucking superhero."

"Honor's mine, Tarek."

∽

IT's deja vu as I walk into HQ for the last time.

Just like the first, no one see's what's coming and no one will try to stop me until it's too late. Unlike the first time, I'm not packing tranqs, and I sure as fuck won't be talking my way out of the consequences.

My mind is racing a mile a minute, and I have to keep looking down at myself to make sure my body's doing what I want it to. I'm so jacked up, it's a constant effort just to make sure I look human. Seems to be working so far, though I'm not sure how.

I don't make eye contact with anyone. A faceless Elite steps into my path, but I push past as I mutter something about being late.

I'm a little disappointed that the blue-haired Dawn isn't at her station today. It'd sure be nice to absorb a little confidence from that smile of hers. Not that it matters now.

Thankfully, my comm works on the second try, and it's smooth sailing up to the top floor. When I walk into the domed room at the top of the building, the final piece falls into place.

Only four Elders are here to meet me, which means my message to Tobias and Tanikka to keep clear was heeded. I wasn't entirely sure they'd all show up, or at least question my reason for wanting to meet in this room. The only room in the building with bulletproof walls.

It's almost too easy.

Even if I had the mental clarity to reconsider my actions, it wouldn't change anything now. Time slows just a bit as I count the steps until I'm less than twenty paces from where they stand.

"Elite Gideon?" Elder Joseph tips his head to the side, his hand reaching for his pocket.

I doubt I can aim for shit with the mess I'm in, but it won't matter.

I haul the twin automatics from their holsters on my thighs. My left arm's a little slower on the draw, but still up to the task. Only Elder Samuel's eyes register what's coming before I let the bullets rain.

Her name is my battle cry.

Glass shatters around me like hail. A blast of air knocks me off my feet, and as my body hits the floor, my vision fills with brilliant green scales.

FIGHTING CHANCE

"*I* did this."

"No, don't say that."

Whisper places her hand on my knee, as I curl tighter into the fetal position. She's perched stiffly on the edge of my bed, and I can feel the tension rolling off her.

"I had the chance to kill her. I knew it needed to happen. I tried. But I let her live. And now Gideon..." Fresh sobs rip from my chest as I remember how he looked. His beautiful body. His gentle strength. "We were going to settle this peacefully. We were going to get married-"

"Married?" Whisper's surprise only makes me angrier. How could we have been so stupid to think that something so simple could solve all this?

"It seems silly now. But I love him... we could have shown everyone."

"It's time to call them home, Hope. All of them."

I nod, wiping the tears from my cheeks and sniffling as I force myself to sit up and think about more than just myself and my loss.

"Do you think so?"

"Yes. They know where we are, or at least roughly where we are, so it's too late to worry about giving away our position. Gideon said the Elders want all Shifters eliminated. We can't assume they won't follow through. Just reach as many as you can. Convince them to hurry."

"I can't connect with the unawakened."

"We'll save the ones we can."

I nod, because that's what it's come to. Saving them all isn't a possibility anymore, if it ever was.

I close my eyes, sinking into the Darkness that was once so terrifying, but now feels like home. I feel nothing here; no grief, anger or love. I only feel them, us, We. I touch them all, offering comfort or courage where it's needed. Time has no meaning in this place, as I drift nowhere and everywhere at once.

I send out the call; a summons they will understand even if they've never heard of me. I try to reach the unawakened, but their sparks are so dim, so cold, I can only offer the smallest connection.

I linger, reluctant to return to the sensations of my own body and heart. But they need me there, and so I go.

I open my eyes and grit my teeth against a rush of emotions. The anger outweighs the sorrow for the moment, and I lean into it.

"Did you call them?"

"I did."

I called them, but I don't know if it was the right thing to do. They aren't safe in the cities, but if we draw more attention here, is this place any safer? What will we do if we don't have the sanctuary of the Meadow?

I feel Damon's approach and we rush to meet him as he touches down. He's been gone for hours, searching for any sign of approaching danger. While I'm confident he would have reached out through our new connection if he'd found anything, I'm still eager to hear it in person.

My heart races when I sense Tarek in the distance. I'd give anything to see Gideon sitting in the saddle; whole and strong. But it can't be possible. Even with his Medic, even with the best medical care, I just don't know.

Damon shifts out of his phoenix. "There's no sign of anyone else approaching that I can see."

Tarek appears over the trees in a hawk form. He shifts as he lands, and even though it's pointless, I hold my breath in hope that he's bringing good news.

"The Elders are dead. All except for Tanikka and Tobias."

I can't even comprehend what he's saying, let alone form a response.

"What the fuck?" Whisper grabs my arm.

I know what she's thinking. If the Elders that wanted Shifters enslaved or dead are gone... so is the threat. All of it... no control, no experiments, no- "Where's Gideon?"

Tarek can't seem to look at me, but he locks eyes with Whisper. "He hit three shots of Medic and suited up."

Whisper gasps, covering her mouth with both hands. I don't know what Tarek means, but I know any last sliver of hope is a futile emotion.

"He was a fucking machine. They never saw him coming."

"Where is he?" Whisper asks.

"I left him at Kelsey's. Didn't know what else to do."

"They'll blame you for it, too."

"Yeah, well, I wasn't going to let him die in custody."

"You could have brought him here." The place where my heart was is now an empty, aching chasm. It's all my fault.

"No. He'd never have wanted me to chance them connecting him with the Meadow. He wouldn't..." Tarek's voice cracks, and he clears his throat before continuing. "He wouldn't have lasted long enough to get here, anyway. I flew to ground, then stole a car to get us to the bar."

It's not fair. Gideon's an Elite, a hero, a Protector. A good man. He deserves so much more than to die a fugitive, taking his last breaths in the back of a bar.

I don't want to cry anymore. I want to destroy something.

"He gave us a fighting chance. Let's not waste it."

They all look at me as if they're shocked by my reaction. I won't break because of this. Not yet. Gideon never quit. Not after all the loss he endured. Right to the end... he never stopped fighting. His mate won't, either.

"Hope, you can take a minute..." Whisper's hand is still on my arm, but I shrug out of her reach.

"No. Whisp, you have a comm?"

"Yeah... haven't turned it on since I got here though."

"Good. Get some distance from the Meadow and find a contact for Dr. Chambers. I want to meet her. Now. Doesn't matter where, as long as Damon can drop me safely."

THE CLICK of heels pulls me away from the Darkness. The chill of the pavement has barely seeped through my pants, even though I spent what seemed like hours in that beautiful place.

I touched each of them. Not only the Meadow residents and the Shifters in the city, but others I hadn't even known existed. Our story is so much bigger than I could have imagined.

A part of me is howling, begging, clawing to escape and stop what I'm about to do. I don't care. I look toward the Solar, the invisible bubble of its atmosphere now tinted red. Sirens wail in the distance. Gideon sacrificed everything to give us a real chance. I'll do nothing less.

"Hope." Marilyn's voice is pleasant, cheery even. As if

we're old friends meeting after too long apart. The smile on her face does little to hide the dark circles under her eyes, or the wrinkle in her clothes as they flutter in the wind.

"Vi is dead, but I assume you know that already."

She raises her chin, even as her smile fades to a frown.

"Yes. I know."

"I hear it's rough to lose your bondmate."

She doesn't answer, but her eyes say plenty. Whatever loss she feels, she'll get over it. Not like bonded Shifters, who die when they lose their human bondmates.

My hand shakes only a little as I pull Vi's gift out of my pocket. The thin syringe is nearly weightless in my palm, but as heavy as forever on my heart. I don't need to explain a thing. Marilyn's eyes widen as she realizes what I came here to do.

"You wouldn't..."

"Have you learned nothing?"

"No!" She screams as she lunges toward me, but it's too late. I've always been a natural at finding a vein, and this particular poison hardly requires accuracy.

She grabs it out of my hand a second too late, then slaps me hard enough to make me stumble. I don't resist, just let myself fall as cold fire spreads through my veins.

I close my eyes, seeing nothing but my eyelids. When I open them again, Marilyn is sitting on the pavement beside me.

"You're a fool."

"We're just people. Let us-" I take a deep breath, looking around me at the shadowed edges of the vacant parking lot. I see the black of Damon's panther, hidden to anyone who doesn't know where to look. Whisp's there too, though I can't see her. Tarek's circling overhead, as inconspicuous as any other bird looking for human scraps. "Let them live."

"This isn't over. I'll find another way. I'll start from scratch, I'll-"

"Good luck with that, because I have a feeling your funding is about to be cut."

I stand up, brushing the dirt off my pants as I turn to go.

"How could you do it? How could you give up that power?"

"It was never about power, that's what people like you can't understand. I was..."

There's no point in explaining anything to her. I walk away, and she doesn't try to stop me. I'm useless to her now.

There is no Alpha.

When I step out of the sun and into the dank space between buildings, Damon pulls me into his arms. "What the hell just happened?"

I soak up his heat and his strength, burrowing into his embrace and wishing it were Gideon's arms around me.

"She killed the Alpha gene." Whisper answers for me.

She must have been able to sense the moment our connection ended. I should have warned her, but I couldn't bring myself to say it out loud. I couldn't risk losing my nerve.

"How is that even possible?" Tarek's voice comes from behind me.

I push away from Damon. "I need to see Gideon."

Tarek nods. "I'll go with you."

"You two can run ahead." Whisper says. "But be careful. By the look of the Solar, they're in full lockdown. It's just a matter of time before they order the same here."

I suck in an unsteady breath and shake my head. "I didn't kill the Alpha gene. I... I can't shift anymore."

The silence stretches, and I can't look at any of them.

"No..."

"Another human weapon. Fitting that it was used to take away the weapon they wanted most." I smile at the irony.

"Is it temporary?" Damon asks.

I'm sure the thought of never being able to shift again is

hard for him to imagine. I've been imagining it since I saw the contents of Vi's pouch.

She knew what needed to happen, whichever one of us survived. If she'd brought two, we could have both taken it. Maybe she could only get her hands on one, or she just didn't want me to be Alpha either way. I guess I'll never know what she was thinking in the end.

"No. It's not." I put my chin up, bracing myself for the pity in Damon's eyes as I look at him.

Defective. A Shifter that can't shift. But this time, it was my choice.

"Take me to Kelsey's."

PROTECTORS

I never expected to be here again.

Even standing at the back door, Kelsey's bar feels a little like coming home. I wait impatiently as Tarek pounds a heavy fist against the door.

Damon has his arm around Hope, offering her what comfort he can. She's barely holding it together. My heart breaks for what she's lost. And for Gideon, who only had a glimpse of the kind of love he deserved.

I hate that we're here to say goodbye. I hate that everything is finally coming together, yet seems to be falling apart at the same time. But in the midst of the grief around me, a piece of my heart beats with anticipation as the door finally opens, and Kelsey steps out into the shade of the building.

Her eyes fall on Tarek first. "Can you help him?"

Hope gasps. "Is he..."

"He's too stubborn to quit, but it's not looking good. He threatened me with creatively violent consequences if I called an ambulance."

"Call one. Now." Hope's voice is a clear order.

"I did, sort of. I know a nurse who will be discrete. He did what he could, but..."

"Where is he?" Hope grabs Tarek by the hand and pulls him along behind her as Kelsey directs them to her office.

When they're gone, she turns to Damon and I, her blue eyes brimming with tears. "Whisper?"

I smile, even though it feels foreign after all that's happened today. In the space of a heartbeat, she's wrapped around me. I hug her tight, and she clings to me like she might never let me go. Then she pushes me back to arm's length and rakes her eyes over me.

"Hey, Kelsey."

"Holy shit."

"I'm so sorry. I wanted to tell you."

She stares at me in silence for a few moments longer, then brushes her fingers down my cheek. Damon slides a possessive arm around my waist, and Kelsey laughs as she swipes the tears off her face.

"Stand down, pussycat. I won't steal your girl."

Damon growls, and I don't know how I keep from laughing at him, but somehow I stifle the urge and pat him on the belly instead.

"You've done amazing things here, Kelsey. Opening this place for Shifters was a risky move, but thank you."

She snorts like it's no big deal. "It was the least I could do. But you... honey, you took down Horizon Zero and half the Elders. You should be a hero, not a deceased fugitive."

"The afterlife isn't so bad." I glance up at Damon, and he gives me a look that reminds me I'm the luckiest woman in the world.

"I can't believe you're alive. I guess Gideon finished what you started." Her face pinches as her chin quivers. "He's become a friend, Whisp. I care about him." Fresh tears spill down her cheeks.

"What he did, him and Hope, it changes everything again. We can..." I look up at Damon.

"What are you thinking?" He crosses his arms, ready to argue whatever plan I'm hatching.

"I'm thinking about everything Hope and Gideon just accomplished, and how they've given us the opportunity to do so much more." I chew on my lower lip, trying to make sense of what I'm proposing. "I think we should go say hello to Tanikka."

Instead of telling me how crazy I am, Damon just shakes his head and sighs, as if he knows he's lost this argument before it even began. Smart man. "Tired of hiding in the woods already?" A sexy half smile joins the spark in his eyes.

He's not conceding anything, because he was already thinking the same thing.

"Not at all. And you know how much I enjoy training the young men and women..." I let that trail off, just to make him squirm.

"Why put yourself at risk again?" Kelsey asks, voicing the argument I assumed Damon would make. "You're safe, and obviously happy. You deserve to enjoy that."

"The Shifter program is all but dead, but I don't want Shifters to fade into stories people tell their kids when they get too close to Morwood." I point at the Solar, that ominous red tint making it look even more other-worldly. "I don't want fear and terrorism to be our legacy. We're Protectors. No matter what they say about the things we did, we've only been protecting the people who need us most."

"So, we're going to ask for our jobs back?"

"Fuck, yeah." I put a hand on my belly, letting him know I'm not forgetting the most important thing we have to protect. I offered everything when Hope said it would save them, but I don't think I'd have the courage to risk that ever again. "Maybe not you and I. We have too much to do back at the Meadow. But other Shifter Protectors, the ones who want to keep working, keep building on this."

"A partnership," Kelsey says, her eyes lighting up.

"It's not good enough to end the corruption. We need to build something better in its place."

Humans and Shifters working together. That sounds really good.

I've travelled farther than most. I've seen a glimpse of what's out there; the vastness and diversity of worlds beyond ours. I thought that kind of perspective would make this place feel small and unimportant. Instead, it's shown me how precious it all is. We have a long way to go if we want a culture of equality and opportunity, but I can see it now.

Most importantly, I can see the role I need to play to achieve it. And I'm so fucking ready.

FAR BETTER

I'm not dead. I'm also not entirely sure I'm conscious, because being in Kelsey's office makes zero sense.

I wait, expecting the apparition to fade and become a jail cell or guarded hospital room, but nothing changes. I grit my teeth as my body protests, but I manage to sit up after a few pathetic tries.

I'm on Kelsey's cot. Naked under the blankets with an IV running into my arm. There's medical equipment around the room and a few chairs. Kelsey's desk is gone. A glass of water sits on a stand beside me, and after a few fumbles I manage to get most of it in.

My stomach lurches when I look down at the ugly, fresh scars that cover my torso. I throw off the sheets and thank sweet fuck none of her claws landed near the junk.

The IV burns as I tug it out of my arm, pushing up to my feet only to sit back down as a bitch of a head rush nearly knocks me out again. A few more tries, and then I'm pulling on the clothes I find neatly folded at the foot of the bed.

Just as I step toward the door, it swings open and I'm

looking into the most beautiful violet eyes I've ever seen. We stare at each other, her face mirroring the awe I feel.

I never thought I'd see her again. I sure as fuck never thought I'd get the chance to hold her again.

"Hope." My voice is as rough as gravel.

She launches herself at me, almost knocking me off my feet as she wraps her arms around me. She feels like heaven. I drink in her scent, her heat, her heart beating against mine. How was there ever a time in my life when I didn't love this woman?

She pulls away, gripping my face in her hands and looking into my eyes with a wild expression on her face.

"Gideon?"

"Yeah... last I checked."

"I thought I lost you." Her eyes brim with tears as her chin quivers.

"Never." I kiss her forehead, her cheeks, her lips.

The door swings wide, and everyone I care about in the world files in.

"Hey! Look who's not brain dead!" Tarek's voice booms in my ears. He slaps me on the arm, then catches me by the shoulders as I stumble on my feet. "Shit, sorry G."

Damon's arms are around Whisper as they both look at me with huge smiles on their faces. Kelsey is wiping tears from her cheeks. Hope is running her hands over me like she still can't believe I'm alive.

I put my hand on my chest. My heart's beating way too fast to be dead, but I'm still uncertain any of this is real.

"What the fuck happened?"

"You didn't die." Tarek offers, and I remember the flash of green scales I saw right before I blacked out.

"No shit. And you didn't get the fuck out like I told you to."

He shrugs, and I've never had the urge to kiss a man before, but I wrap my arm around his thick neck and plant one on his forehead.

"Fuck, G." He pulls out of my grip, wiping his brow and failing at looking pissed. "Hope's the one you should be thanking."

"What did you do?"

"She gave you a transfusion," Whisp says. "It was a long shot, but apparently Shifter blood is powerful in their bond-mate's veins."

"Transfusions. Plural." Tarek adds. "I'm sure she would have bled me dry if it would have upped your odds."

I just stare at Hope in awe of everything she is, and she stares right back at me. I see myself through her eyes, the pure joy in just the fact that I'm still here. How did I get so fucking lucky?

"What happened? Are we safe for now?"

"I've been talking to Tanikka and Tobias." Whisper says. "They're claiming an assassin killed the other Elders, and you two brought him down. There's been so many lies supporting the Shifter program, they agreed one last lie to end it won't hurt. It's the only free pass we'll get, though. They're committed to moving forward with honesty and transparency."

That sounds damn good to me. Too damn good.

"Hope called the awakened Shifter's to the Meadow," Damon says. "All Shifter programs are on hold for review, and I think it's safe to say we'll be seeing some big changes."

"Goddamnit, guys. I can't believe it fucking worked." Did I seriously survive this, and without a prison sentence? It's surreal. "What about Dr. Chambers? Is she out of the picture? Even with the changes in government policy, I can't ima-"

The expression that crosses everyone's face makes me swallow my words. They all turn to Hope, and the look on her face makes my stomach turn. What did she do?

"Can I talk to him alone?" Her voice is barely a whisper, but they all jump to give us space. Tarek gives me another, gentler, slap on the shoulder before he leaves, closing the door behind him.

"What did you do?"

She threads her fingers behind my head and pulls me down into a kiss that makes me even more certain I've died and gone to some place far better than I deserve. When she pulls away, we're both out of breath and I've confirmed that, yep, junk's still working just fine.

Fuck, I'd love to lay her down right now... but I need a shower and an hour-long piss before I can give her what she deserves. Instead, I settle for wrapping my arms around her and holding her tight against me.

"Tell me everything."

MY HOPE

I close my eyes as I listen to the steady, strong beat. It's the most beautiful sound I've ever heard.

Damon and Whisper are hand in hand as they stare in awe at the ultrasound screen. Tears glisten in Damon's eyes as he looks from the tiny new life on the display, to the woman at his side. I'm struck with a wave of gratitude at the honor of being witness to this moment.

His expression is one of pure, unwavering love. When they kiss, I turn off the machine and give them some privacy.

The clinic is my heart. It's my home. It always has been, even though I may have doubted it for a while. But even after everything that's happened, my connection with my people through my work here remains as strong as it always was.

I'm not their Alpha. But I'm honored to call myself their doctor, and their friend.

I'll be needing help around here soon. The young are keeping me busy enough; sixteen little souls, mercifully liberated from the lab and entrusted to us by the Elders. They have a future now. A family.

In addition to the herd of pups, kittens and cubs is the flow of new arrivals that's continued to increase in the weeks since I sent out the call. They're not just coming from Moridian, they're coming from places we never knew existed. I saw it all so plainly when I could travel in the Darkness.

The Meadow might be the biggest free Shifter community, but the forest is vast. The Shifters of Morwood number far more than we ever imagined. We have no need for the convenience and comforts of the human cities. The forest is our home.

The future's as promising as it is uncertain. I'm ready for whatever role I'm needed to fill.

But for now, I have the overwhelming urge to burrow into the arms of a certain someone who's shown me what true love feels like.

I slip out of the clinic tent, and he's already waiting for me. He scoops me up without hesitation and kisses me until I can't remember my own name.

"Ready to go?" He asks when we catch our breath.

"Gideon, you know this isn't necessary. It seems silly... all this fuss about a piece of paper."

"I don't care. No matter how much you protest. I said I wanted to marry you, and I meant it."

"But I-"

"Hope, will you marry me?"

I huff an exaggerated sigh and roll my eyes. "For the hundredth time, yes."

"Then stop arguing and let's go. Tanikka's waiting."

I look up at him, basking in the pure joy on his face as he looks back at me. I touch the scars on his neck. They're faint now, only slightly pink. They cover his chest and belly like a map I love to follow with my tongue, reminding us both of the pleasure his pain made possible.

I'll always mourn the loss of the connection I had with my

people. The loss of the freedom to feel the wind in my fur, my paws against the earth, my voice mingling with the calls of the wild wolves in the moonlight.

But I have no regrets. Not one. The connection and freedom I found in this man's arms is worth any sacrifice. My nightmares are nothing compared to the new dreams he's given me.

"You sure we don't have a few minutes to spare?"

His eyes blaze at my insinuation.

He takes my face in his big hands, kissing me in that gentle yet fierce way that never ceases to take my breath away. Then he grabs me by the hand and I'm laughing as he leads the way to our tent.

SHE PUSHES me back toward the cot, her expression predatory as she peels her shirt over her head. I don't waste a second pulling my clothes off. When she gets that look in her eyes, she's every bit my wolf. She may not be able to take that form anymore, but she's still the powerful, beautiful creature I met at the lake.

She pins me down, biting my neck as she straddles my hips. When she lowers herself onto me, we both sigh with the pure, perfect bliss of being exactly where we belong.

She rides me slowly, head tipped back and lips parted. I love watching her face. I love hearing the sounds of her pleasure even as she tries to stay quiet. Most of all, I love that we never have to stop. She's mine.

The languorous pace is delicious, but we both crave more.

Soon, she's grinding into me with a frenzied rhythm as I grip her hips. When I can't wait a second longer, I flip her onto her back and take her with everything I've got. I know it's the way she wants it, the way she loves it, and I'll damn well give her all the pleasure she can handle.

My lover. My mate. My wife.

She tries her best to muffle the sounds of her orgasm... both of them... but when I come, I don't give a shit who hears. I should be dead, but instead I'm in the arms of the woman I love. And I'm coming so fucking hard.

Hope laughs until she cries as she tries in vain to cover my roars with her hands over my mouth.

She's still laughing when we tangle ourselves together and bask in the aftershocks of the most incredible love I've ever felt.

"I love you, Gideon."

I run my hands over her back, kissing her hair as she does the same to my chest.

"I love you, my Hope."

∼

CURIOUS TO KNOW what's next?

SPARKS FLY when Tarek meets the woman who makes his dragon purr. Can the man measure up to the myth, or will she slip through his fingers forever?

FIND OUT NOW, in *Dawn in the Shadows*!

A NOTE FROM THE AUTHOR

Thank you for reading Hope and Gideon's story!

Would you like to hear about my future releases and be the first to get freebies and sneak peeks? Subscribe to my newsletter at www.CharlenePerry.ca

If you enjoyed this book, please consider leaving a review wherever you can. As an indie author, reviews are critical for helping my books find the readers who will love them. I adore hearing what you think of my work. It gives me confidence, motivates me to push through the hard parts, and inspires me to keep adding to the series you love!

For more information about me or my stories, be sure to check out my website! (www.charleneperry.ca)

Find me on Facebook! @CharlenePerryAuthor. I love to chat and am always delighted to receive feedback :)

Thank you so much for spending this time with me,

Sweet Dreams!
  -Charlene

SNEAK PEEK...

"You won't let anything happen to me."

He steps closer, and I hold my breath as he leans in close, his hand brushing my hair as his warm breath caresses my ear.

"I don't want him to know what it feels like to be this close to you. I don't want him to know that you smell like strawberries and mint, or that you hold your breath when you're nervous."

Holy hell.

I let my breath out slowly.

I can feel the heat from his body. His breath is on my cheek as his fingers trail down the side of my neck.

I turn my head, inhaling his smokey scent as I brush my lips against his. He sucks in a breath. When he doesn't move, I trail the tip of my tongue along the seam of his mouth.

He growls, a low rumble that starts deep in his chest and moves upward until I feel the vibration on my lips.

"You shouldn't do that."

"Why not?"

His eyes meet mine, the emerald flashing. "I'm a Shifter."

My chest constricts. It couldn't have been easy for him to

hear that conversation with Daniel. I know I'm a good liar. It's part of the job, really. Carrying on conversations about topics I have no interest in, pretending to like sports teams I've never heard of or movies I've never watched. I've never considered it dishonest. I like to make people feel comfortable.

"I know you're a Shifter." I reach up and touch my fingertips to his lips, brushing them along his stubbled jaw and down his neck. "You're incredible."

His lids drift shut as he rests his forehead against mine. He is incredible. He's also beautiful, kind, and the sexiest man I've ever laid eyes on.

"I've never wanted a female like this before."

I shudder at his words. The way he whispers them, like a confession. The way he uses the word *female*. It's so raw, so pure.

"I want you, too."

He pulls his head back, meeting my eyes.

Then his mouth is on mine. His kiss starts with a sweetness that makes me melt into him, then turns demanding. He grips my hips, pulling me tight against him as he presses me to the wall. The evidence of his arousal presses into my stomach, and I practically claw at his shirt, desperate to see more of him, to feel more of him.

My comm buzzes in my pocket. I'm more than happy to ignore it, but Tarek freezes. He grips my wrists, stopping my fumbling attempt to get his clothes off.

"You should see who it is."

"I don't care who it is."

He grins, tipping his head to brush a soft kiss over my cheek. "If it's Tanikka, ignoring her will have an Agent at your door in five minutes."

I groan, but he releases my hands and I check the screen. My stomach drops.

"It's him." I hate to even say the words.

Tarek growls, his hands balling into fists. "You don't need to do this."

I slide my thumb across the screen and put the comm to my ear. Because I do have to do this.

I am doing this.

"Hello?"

~

Read *Dawn in the Shadows*, available now!